Where She Went

stories

Kate Walbert

These are uncorrected advance proofs bound for your
reviewing convenience. Please check with the publisher
or refer to the finished book whenever you are
excerpting or quoting in a review.

Sarabande  Books

LOUISVILLE, KENTUCKY

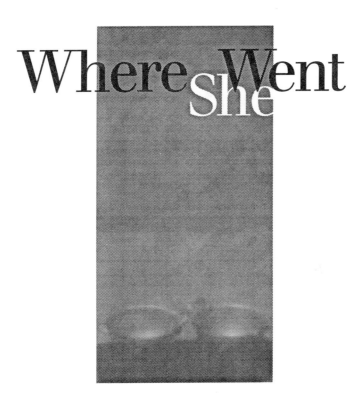

Where She Went

stories

Kate Walbert

Sarabande Books

LOUISVILLE, KENTUCKY

Managing Editor
Sarabande Books, Inc.
2234 Dundee Road, Suite 200
Louisville, KY 40205

LIBRARY OF CONGRESS CATALOGING-IN-PUBLICATION DATA

Walbert, Kate, 1961–
    Where she went : stories / by Kate Walbert. — 1st ed.
        p.   cm.
    ISBN 1-889330-15-9 (alk. paper)
    I. Title.
    PS3573.A42113W47   1998
    813' .54—dc21   97-32195
                                                                        CIP

Cover Photograph: "Small Blue Offering" by Maggie Taylor. Used by kind permission.

Cover and text design by Charles Casey Martin.

Manufactured in the United States of America.
This book is printed on acid-free paper.

Sarabande Books is a nonprofit literary organization.

For my mother and father,
and for Rafael

ACKNOWLEDGMENTS

Some of these stories were originally published in somewhat different form in the following magazines: *The Paris Review, DoubleTake, Press, Fiction, Antioch Review, StoryQuarterly, The Laurel Review, Whispering Campaign,* and *TO: A Journal of Poetry and Prose.*

Grateful acknowledgment is made to the Connecticut Commission on the Arts, the Yaddo Corporation, and the MacDowell Colony for support during the writing of these stories.

CONTENTS

Paris, 1991

‹ 13 ›

MARION

Niagara Falls, 1955

‹ 29 ›

New York, 1954

‹ 35 ›

Tokyo, 1963

‹ 55 ›

Rochester, 1965

‹ 63 ›

Norfolk, 1966

‹ 73 ›

A Place on a Lake, 1966

‹ 87 ›

Baltimore, 1975

‹ 101 ›

REBECCA

Jamaica, 1978

‹ 111 ›

Florence, 1980

‹ 119 ›

Guiseppe, 1988

‹ 127 ›

New York, 1988

‹ 155 ›

Istanbul, 1990

‹ 165 ›

Ithaca, 1992

‹ 175 ›

The Author

‹ *199* ›

Should we have stayed at home
and thought of here?
Where should we be today?
　　　　—Elizabeth Bishop
　　　　"Questions of Travel"

Paris

1991

Into the city of light she descends in darkness. Or this is how Rebecca hears it: I descend on the city of light in darkness. A gray storm-ridden sky, clouds bunched in fat grape colors, a strange mauve. The city of stone streaked with pigeon shit, ripped rock-and-roll posters. A poet's place.

Rebecca cannot see but imagines the inside of all the passing storefronts: cafés, restaurants, boutiques where, she has heard, they arrange the clothing by color.

Crowds on narrow sidewalks herd beneath umbrellas, everyone wearing smart raincoats. Parisians.

"Did you ask him?" she asks Tom. "Does he know where to go?"

"He knows," Tom says. He does not look at her. She turns away to the taxi window. Paris, she thinks. The name is enough. Round as a bun, the "P." Marie Antoinette. The South, something about cake. Tanks barreling through the Arc de Triomphe. Springtime. Poplar blooms. Or maybe, winter. She can't remember. She studied French once, with a teacher who wore red wool dresses and clunky shoes.

Mademoiselle, they called her. The boys with CB radios, the girls in cheerleading uniforms: *Mademoiselle,* they said, blowing smoke rings. *Merde,* they said in the hallways. It's time for French.

I'm hungry," Rebecca says out the window, though she hears Tom's light snoring. The taxi moves slowly over a bridge, and, in the instant before it bumps onto a narrow street, she glimpses a long gray river and silver church domes of unimaginable heights.

They have come to this city from New York to create a baby. A baby in the city of light, Rebecca said. How can that not be possible? It is the right time, more or less. She has packed her thermometer. In the books, the woman registers the same temperature at ten o'clock every morning, except for one, when the mercury line rises point six degrees.

"Point six degrees," she told Tom, zipping up. "That's what we're looking for."

Tom wakes from his nap and stretches his arms, touching walls on both sides papered the color of weak tea. Water stains map the ceiling. The pillows smell of spiderwebs and sweet perfume. Rebecca opens the shutters, the glass doors of the window. Dust on her fingers, a tangerine glint to the rain. Orange light reflected in tiny tears; what had she heard? That insects fly through a downpour without getting wet. No insects here. No screens. Only flowerpots and wrought iron and five-story buildings painted the color of old teacups and women with black hair and the sound: a crowd far away, pushing at the seams of quiet. Someone nearby coughs. Spits. Rebecca leans farther out the window. "You can see the gate to the place des Vosges," she says, bending at the waist. She wears panties and a bra, her white skin mottled pink from cold, from rain. She sits back down on the corner of the tiny bed and puts on her stockings.

"Who told you about this place?" Tom says.

"I read it," Rebecca says. She checks her stockings for runs, spreads a leg over five fingers, hand webbed black. "They said it was in the heart of the romantic district. Look," she says. "Quack, quack."

They walk in the rain; there is nothing else to do. She would like to tell him certain things, what she has done or imagined she has done before this moment in her life, but every time she opens her mouth to start a conversation she feels tired. She had thought that to be in Paris with a husband meant to be bent, head to head, in discussion.

They wear long underwear, coats, and sweaters. Tom is unshaven: blond curly hair, face speckled with gray beard. She holds his hand. He holds an umbrella. She imagines them old; she imagines them closer to the end of their life. We are already old, she thinks.

They walk up the flat gray steps leading into the Bibliothèque Nationale, into the galleries. In a dark and crowded room, illuminated manuscripts. Boxed in plastic. Yellow as jellyfish. Glowing. Devils swoon on every page, sharp-eared men with pointy noses, tiny fingernails, hovering on the shoulders of gentle women; knights, whispering Latin curses. The colors, dyes pounded from berries and bark, bleed from other centuries' rainstorms, floods, natural disasters, Rebecca reads. People in raincoats push at her, stepping close to the plastic boxes, their collective breath hot, steamy. Everyone reads a brochure, or listens to tapes hung around their necks.

Outside, the rain has stopped. Clouds blow against the sun, people appearing like swimmers underwater, dappled, squinting, slow moving. Rebecca and Tom join the tide, pushing along the sidewalk, looking for a café that looks romantic. On the street, they talk of their baby, how their baby could not help but come in a city like this. What baby wouldn't want parents who roamed the world?

"Do you think they really choose?" Rebecca asks.

"What do you mean?" Tom says

"Babies. You've heard that before. I've told you that before. That there's some theory that the baby chooses its parents, decides who it wants to be born to, who it likes."

He looks at her. She shrugs. "It makes sense," she says.

"You would have chosen Marion?"

"Well, what did I know?" she says. "I wasn't even born."

A waitress leads them to a table in the back, near a group of four old men playing cards. A cane is propped against the wall, mustard yellow, fissures thin as hairs. "Look," Rebecca says, pointing at them. "It's like we're in a painting."

She orders goat cheese and arugula, a glass of red wine. Tom orders oysters. To get him in the mood, he says. They sit with their hands entwined; they have nothing to say.

Paris 1991

"Oh dear," Rebecca says, turning her face away from him to look out the big glass windows. "The city of light's gone dark."

They came to Paris impromptu; this is how Rebecca would tell it. In truth, they came to find conversation, a way of being two together. Lately, Rebecca, taller than Marion, with thin, gray streaks in her hair, has begun to resemble her father, Robert. She feels distracted always, often alone. She would like to run through a rainstorm or hunt big game somewhere. Marion has been dead for months, her death quick and cruel, the cancer undetected, her organs gone spongy and blue. Rebecca often sees her: in doorways, crossing the street. She is like all the women whose lives have given out on them too suddenly.

So Rebecca has decided to live in the moment. No regrets, no sorrow. Only the next day and the next. This decision happened on a night when Tom pulled her down to the kilim that covers the wide plank floors of their apartment. Rebecca stood and walked to their bedroom closet, to the drawer where she kept her diaphragm, its hard plastic case the color of a prosthesis. Normally, she would have crouched down on the closet floor to insert it. But this time she carried it out to him, ceremoniously, after first finding a pair of scissors in the kitchen.

"Are you watching closely?" she said. "This is a moment."

"Are you sure?" Tom said.

"No, but why not?" she said, cutting the diaphragm in half. She held the two pieces as if debating whether they could be glued back together, then walked back into the kitchen to throw them in the trash. Tom wrapped his sweater around his waist and followed her.

"We should talk about this," he said.

She sat at the kitchen table.

"We should talk," he said again.

"We have," she said. "Anyway, there's no good time, really, is there? I mean, you either do it or you don't. And we know we don't want to don't, so we might as well do, right?"

"But are you sure?" he said.

"Look at this," Rebecca says, showing Tom the postcard of devils she had bought earlier in the Bibliothèque gift shop. "Marion would have loved this. I could have sent it with a note, Having a devilish good time. She'd think we were running nude in fountains or something."

Tom takes the postcard, pushing his eyeglasses down his nose to see clearly.

Rebecca thinks of Marion and Robert, traveling to New Zealand, returning to paste photographs in one of the albums they received each year for Christmas.

She finishes her wine. Behind her, the four men argue, their voices rising. They smell of wet wool and cigarettes, hours spent over yellowing cards.

"The picture reminded me of something, of some poem I remember reading in school. Blake, I'm sure."

"I thought he was the one with the chimney sweeps," Tom says.

She shrugs. "Anyway, I liked it. Marion would have thought it very cosmopolitan."

Rebecca picks at her wool pants. She is a little drunk, and suddenly the dusk seems to sweep her under a current of melancholy. She thinks of a line she once heard, attributed to Van Gogh. What was it? *Empty chairs—there are many of them,soon there will be more.*

"Poor Marion," she says. "Poor baby."

▼

Paris 1991

That night, Tom lies on the bed, his feet hanging over the edge of the soft mattress, his arms stretched above his head, palms turned and flat against the wall. Rebecca walks across the tiny room in the dark, away from him, to the window. She can see across the street into another room where a woman lights candles on a table, bending over, holding a long tapered match. Red geraniums in clay pots, cobalt blue shutters. It is as if Rebecca looks into a shadowbox: the kitchen leading into the living room leading into the dining room. The woman stands up straight, pausing as if to admire the look of the table with light; then she steps away and walks toward a door.

"Let's go," Rebecca says, turning back to Tom. Long thin legs are the most of him. And elbows. Neck. Large hands. He wears his sneakers. White athletic socks pulled high, almost to his hairy knees.

"Now? It's late," he says.

"The Parisians are just sitting down to dinner. All across the city, the Parisians are sitting down to dinner. Haven't you ever heard the expression 'When in Rome'? For Christ's sake."

She turns away from him, faces the window. The woman's shutters have been drawn closed, though there is still light sifting through them; she imagines the woman coming in from the kitchen now, with some sort of cognac. And pears. There would be ripe, yellow pears, sliced with pearly-handled silver. Heirlooms passed down in worn wooden chests, kept in corners covered in maroon velvet; everything draped with a soft worn fabric documenting a certain tenable history. The woman would bend close to the table as she set down the plate, wooden, that held the yellow pears, and the light might catch the sheen in her black hair, brushed hard every evening the way she had been taught by her mother, who learned from her mother. And so on.

There would also be cheese.

"I don't know. I want some cognac, or a plate of fruit and cheese. Wouldn't that be nice? To just, on a whim, go out close to midnight for a plate of fruit and cheese? For a cognac?"

Tom swings his long legs off the bed. "Sure," he says.

"What will we name it?" Rebecca asks Tom in the morning. They sit in a café across from Saint Sulpice, waiting for the church to open. Somewhere bells ring, and when the trucks go by, the pigeons that roost on the backs of the gargoyles erupt, their wings white and gray-speckled. Rebecca has read that a man who lives across the street grows tomatoes on his roof in the summertime and hands them out to tourists.

Tom looks up from the Herald Tribune, a mustache of milk foam above his lip. "The baby?" he says.

"Of course," she says.

"I don't know," he says, looking back down. "That's bad luck."

"Why?"

"We haven't even, you know. I mean, it could take a year. It could never happen at all."

He pretends to read. She knows better.

"Hello? Hello, monsieur. I'm talking to you."

"I don't like these games."

She feels rebuked, a child. She looks down at the black wool skirt she has put on. When they were in Istanbul last year, she wore the long skirts the books said were required, even though the German tourists went practically nude. Here, she feels dowdy, old, the Parisian women so composed. She wants to buy yards of fabric and sew curtains for every window of their apartment. Yards and yards of tulle, or stiff silk, brilliant yellows and blues. She sees herself sewing, bent over into the night; in the morning she would go to the Korean grocery and buy armloads of tulips.

"Mademoiselle?" Tom says.

She looks up. He has wiped his mouth; the beard he grows on vacations is stiff. A handsome man, she thinks. I have married a handsome man.

"How about Sophie?" he says.

"Sophie? I never would have thought of that."

He shrugs and looks back down at the paper. "I always liked that name," he says.

They enter Saint Sulpice with a few other tourists, a boy with long hair and a guitar case strapped to his back, two elderly women. This bronze meridian line, Tom reads to Rebecca, represents France's nineteenth-century passion for science.

She follows France's passion for science, walking behind Tom. At a certain aisle, he turns toward a rosette and she continues to the famous portrait of the Virgin and child she has read about. The child's face looks like an old man, as if he weren't born a baby but someone who had already lived a life, made up his mind; the Virgin's face looks like a baby's face.

In front of the portrait, long thin white candles burn in a bronze candelabra; what looks like a parking meter has been mounted in front of the candelabra. For three francs, the sign reads in English, anyone can buy another candle to light. The money will be sent to a missionary in Bhutan.

Rebecca counts out her coins and puts them into the meter; then she holds the long thin candle against one of the many flames.

"Poor Marion," she says. "Poor Sophie."

When Rebecca first met Tom, she lived in her studio apartment and he lived in California in a rented house with white stucco walls and a fireplace never used. When he came to New York, they would spend evenings sitting on the couch in her studio, looking out the window to the park across the street. There were trees there, and swingsets, and lights that made the shadows grow to other things. They would play the game she had suggested, a game of imagining their other lives—not past lives, but all the other lives they could have led. I learned this from my mother, she told him.

She could have lived in Florence with a man named Mohammed, or been in the movies with the owner of the place where she stayed in Jamaica. She could have met someone in Rajasthan and ridden elephants. Or lived on the island in Greece where the old widow ran her television on a car battery. Each morning, the widow cooked her an omelet of fresh eggs and goat cheese, browned at the edges. She would sit beneath grapevines looking out to the Aegean, at a wooden table carved with the initials of other visitors. There was a woman who had rented a room for many months, a woman she never saw, though once she had looked through the small window to see someone who sat at a desk, her back turned to the view. The widow said this woman lived in England and had come there alone, though she had a photograph of a child she kept on her desk. Maybe the child died, Rebecca said to the old widow.

Maybe she has run away, the old widow said back.

Tom had listened and then said that he could have been a passenger on the train that crossed Canada, but that recently they disconnected the route.

Despite this, she fell in love with him, first falling in love with his name: Tom, a big "T" and little "o" and an "m." Sounded good in her mouth when she said it: I'll be dining with Tom this evening. Tom and I are going out. Tom thinks this. Tom Tom Tom Tom Tom. Mot, backwards. Tom was in a difficult relationship. Tom had had a bad time of it.

People liked Tom. They liked his big hands and his little glasses and the way he would play the guitar at parties and the way he always sang a song he wrote at college. No one really understood the words, but they found it quaint.

When she traveled to California, to his town, they would wake up early and hike down to the dock where the boat owners came for eggs. They sat at picnic tables, and Tom would pull apart his soggy bread and throw it up for the seagulls to catch in their gray beaks. This, and a cigarette from time to time, a single bought from the drugstore they would share on the cliffs overlooking the Pacific, the sound of the roller coaster behind them as constant as the surf.

But there seemed a certain adventure in what they had then. In Paris, they both feel awkward, as if they are watched from every window, their actions exaggerated, their voices loud and shrill. They hadn't expected such cold; wool hats hide their faces as they walk, glove in glove, down the Champs Élysées, aware of their numb feet and runny noses, aware of the bare trees.

▼

At dinner, Tom orders champagne, more oysters. The restaurant is cavernous, dark, swelling with the voices of a hundred Frenchmen; some sort of argument seems to have erupted at every table. What is everyone saying? Rebecca asks. Something seems to be going on.

Wine, I think, Tom says. Wine and good food. He seems entirely pleased. He has put on a jacket and a pressed shirt, buttoning the cuffs. His beard looks planned, cultivated, not the result of days unattended. His glasses bright and clean. At times, she finds herself looking at him as if he is entirely unfamiliar to her, a blind date, or somebody's cousin she has agreed to meet.

"What are you thinking?" he says.

"Marion," she says. "I was thinking of how she always spoke of coming to Paris and now here we are." Rebecca looks around her; on the brick wall is a framed print she recognizes: still life with fruit. "I'm trying to imagine her in Paris, actually, and I can't get her kelly green coat out of my mind. I think she would have worn her kelly green coat, and some sort of smart hat, and I think she would have come to the city in better weather, and would have sat out in the cafés and watched the people and met some dashing Frenchman named Monsieur something, who wouldn't have minded her at all."

Tom gestures to the waitress for the check, signing his name in the air. Rebecca looks down at her wool pants.

"I think you're thinking of Audrey Hepburn in *Gigi*," he says. "Marion would have hated the food."

Rebecca does not look at Tom's face, now over her. She can feel him sometimes, his prickly cheek, chin. She tries to think of things other than babies, but they float out to her on clouds, cherubs pink as the angels in the illuminated manuscripts. She feels someone watching; she feels this already, a soul hovering, debating whether to come back into this world.

Beneath the window, she knows, the cobblestones shine wet. She might hear horse hooves, the quiet clopping of a team on their way to the place des Vosges. She imagines a carriage, a woman behind the shuttered carriage windows, her hand gloved in white velvet, her body swathed in fresh silk: a princess, a saint, a mother, a daughter, a goddess borne out of this place to another. There are babies there, and devils, too; they are all of them hovering, waiting to descend, waiting to be asked, waiting for their chance to be born.

MARION

Niagara Falls

1955

The nickname never stuck, although Marion tried it at several angles, starting first when she saw Robert in tennis shorts, his legs like two sticks at the end of each knee, insect things, his black hair rubbed away by his pants in some places, by his socks at the ankles.

Marion said spider was the first thing that came to mind, so she said so.

Marion also said that Robert took it in stride, although perhaps it got to him finally, rubbing off, like the leg hair, after too much contact.

Then Marion told Johnson, Robert's colleague, that Robert had spider legs, and to call him, from now on, Spider. Johnson would drive from Rye every morning, taking the Bear Mountain Parkway through the tunnel and then up, stopping for Robert at the rented house behind the Moorings', where Robert lived now with Marion and where, until recently, he had lived by himself.

Ready at the sound of Johnson's car tires on the gravel, Robert would be out before Johnson had time to honk. Marion had seen to no honking and would stand waiting at the door until they were gone.

"Spider," Johnson said, to show her he had picked up on it, "you drive."

Marion came from the middle of the country, near a Great Lake few could remember the name of. It was common knowledge that she had a temper and that, given the opportunity, would lose herself in a fit so heady that once even the Moorings took the time to come over. It also went that she had Robert completely, to the point where, tiring of the fireplace mantel, she got him to borrow a crowbar from Mr. Mooring, right at that moment, and to rip the thing off entirely, leaving only a web of hanging pieces.

"Things will get to you," Robert said in Marion's defense, perhaps surprised himself at his new wife's temper. These were the days when strangers married, Marion would tell her daughter, Rebecca, vis-à-vis how she, Marion, could have ended up with a man so entirely unlike her—a man of routine, precision, a company man who made her lose her temper, who got her so mad she could spit.

Just twenty, Marion had arrived in New York City six months before finding herself set up for tennis doubles with an unknown Robert Clark, a man then so enamored of the color of her hair that he lost his serve foolishly before regaining his poise.

She was the younger of two sisters who married one after the other in the month of June. She was the first, driving away from her parents' farm in Robert's red convertible, which may or may not have played some part in her quick decision.

Regardless, she drove away.

On their honeymoon they visited Niagara Falls and paid for their photograph to be taken underneath one of the many rainbows created by the spray. They stood arm-in-arm, looking more like school chums on a field trip than man and wife. Later, they put on yellow slickers and took the rowboat ride close to the falls. Marion screamed halfway out and confessed to Robert that she had had a momentary vision of the two of them falling, tumbling to the deep in giant underwater somersaults.

She practiced her cooking while Robert was at work and at night kept the radio on, sometimes wanting him to dance with her right there in the kitchen and sometimes sending him away so she could sit alone listening to the music.

Her father, she had told him, was a union leader who had shaken the hand of every president, at least once; her mother, working, too, had let the sisters raise themselves, so the oldest already knew what it was like to mother before marrying, on the second weekend of June. On a drive to Chicago, for instance, their mother had crawled into the backseat, telling her, then eleven, to keep the car between the white lines.

Strangely, Marion said, she had only thought of this story once before, when a kid rubbed his body against hers in the subway and she was held, unable to move, against him.

She began to cook elegantly. For their Thanksgiving party she served Rock Cornish game hens baked in clay, individually, every place set with a small hammer, red ribbons tied around the handles, and name cards in front of the water glasses. On their first Christmas, she made a lamb marinated in mint, a recipe she passed on to Rebecca, written on a blue-lined index card. Robert beamed and asked for seconds. Then he disappeared to find the large box he had wrapped for her the night before. In it were star sapphire earrings and a fox stole with a card reading, *Love, Spider.* He had made up a nickname for her. Magnolia, he thought, would be fine, but she had eventually told him to stop saying it. "Don't be stupid," she said when he persisted.

She needed help with the dining room table. She was sure it was cherry, and they had bought it for a lark. She wanted to shine it up for a party and paint the living room walls parrot green; she was going to paint them a solid, shocking green. "If anyone asks why we did it this color, Spider," she told Robert, "you say it was my idea." She had begun to settle in, Robert told Johnson; there were girls in the neighborhood like herself, friends to be made. Her temper had subsided. She packed his sandwiches in brown paper bags, occasionally adding a note.

He notices her hair is more beautiful outdoors and remarks on it. She complains that their friends think she dyes it; nobody ever believes it is real. He says, Nonsense. He says he's sure no one has ever doubted her. She is simply a beautiful woman, beautiful, he says, and probably understanding.

Understanding? She wants to know how.

Niagara Falls 1955

Of leaving, he says. We've been asked to go. Missouri, really. Are you game?

They will leave by May, the kitchen now so crammed with boxes that when she sits alone listening to the radio she sits in constant shadow. Never mind, Robert says. I won't lose you.

He takes her picture outside on Easter Sunday, after she has pierced the ham with peppercorns and toothpicks, anchoring apples; she is going to let it cook slowly, she says. It needs time to cook. She has on the kelly green coat he let her buy, giving her an extra allowance to cheer her up. She had wanted to put down roots, she said. She had wanted to get her ducks in a row.

Now Marion follows Robert outside and stands next to a tree between their house and the Moorings', hand on one hip and face up, her chin pointing at the sun. She tells him she wants to look directly at the sun so the glare will come off her face; she tells him to make sure he catches the glare in the picture. Reaching up, she pulls down a low branch, pretending she is stepping under it, looking toward the sun as if she is going somewhere and has a place in mind.

In the way that she stands, her new coat open, he can easily see the line of her neck, her hand lifting up, the star sapphires, her face, so that he catches it just right, not paying any attention to her instructions, seeing only her hair and the way the sun picks up the brown as well as the red, making it all a gold sheen.

Then she says, "Robert, come on, I can't hold this forever," and he takes the picture without even knowing that he has shifted the focus, losing her, that suddenly, to the frame.

New York

1954

I left by train. Have I told you? I was nineteen years old, had gone to Indiana State on a scholarship that didn't work out. Twelve dollars in my pocket, I headed for New York City. This was 1954. I wore a hat. And white gloves.

Can you picture me?

In those days people dressed to travel, laid their clothes out the night before and pressed them even. You wouldn't be caught dead without a handkerchief in your handbag. You carried mints. I think I wore a simple dress, very neat. It would have been green, because I always wore green. I looked what they called in those days smart.

I didn't know a thing.

When I arrived at Pennsylvania Station, I dialed an acquaintance of your Aunt Cynthia's. Cynthia said this woman had moved to New York years before, and that, if I got into trouble, I should call her and let her know who I was.

I remember she answered the telephone as if expecting something.

"Yes?" she said.

"Doris?" I said.

"What?" she said.

"It's Marion Prochotska," I said. "Cynthia's little sister. I'm in New York."

"Oh," she said.

I waited a moment. Commuters hurried around me. I'm not sure whether I had ever before been in a room with so many people.

"Marion?" Doris said. "Where are you? Are you on the street? Are you calling from the street?"

"I'm at Pennsylvania Station," I said.

"Oh," Doris said. "Are you going home?"

I laughed. "I just got here," I said. "I'm here. That's why I'm calling."

"You just got here? Oh. Well, come for dinner then. 180th and Wadsworth Avenue. 723 Wadsworth, apartment 4D. Seven o'clock. Come for dinner. We'll have dinner."

I hung up the phone and looked around. 180th and Wadsworth Avenue. I wasn't even sure how to exit Pennsylvania Station.

When I got there, I rang the front buzzer and heard the same woman who had answered the telephone. "Yes?" she said.

"Doris, it's Marion," I said.

"This isn't Doris," she said.

Can you picture me? At that moment, I stood in the vestibule of a run-down tenement in the middle of a city I had no knowledge of, and though I was stupid I was smart enough to be afraid. After all, there I was, less than twelve dollars in my pocket and quite truthfully no idea where I would spend the night. On the subway uptown, I had found myself pinned against a kid who had rubbed his body against mine. I was unable to move and could only think pleasant thoughts. Oddly, I thought of the time Mother had taken Cynthia and me on a trip to Chicago. Halfway there, she pulled over to the side of the road and told Cynthia to drive. Cynthia was eleven. "Just keep the car between the white lines," Mother told her, and crawled to the backseat to nap.

I was almost out the front door when I heard someone behind me. "Marion?" she said.

I turned around. In front of me stood something out of the zoo: leopard skin pants and a long red tunic. She had gold eyeshadow up to her eyebrows and dyed blonde hair piled high in a messy beehive. She was what I had only seen in the movies, a kind of Natalie Wood beatnik.

"Are you Marion?" she said.

"Yes," I said. "Are you Doris?"

"Doris, God, Doris. Don't mention her name in my presence or I'm like to throw a fit. I'm Katherine. Lately considering Kat. Do you like it?"

"I guess," I said.

She looked me over.

"Anyway, Doris isn't here. She left a few weeks ago. Wrote a note. Eloped or something. It's a long story. Come on up."

Katherine opened the door wider for me to walk through. I carried the suitcase I had brought, my dresses folded, tissue leaves dividing one from the other, and bumped past her up the stairs to 4D.

"Go on," she said when I got to the door. "It's open."

I went in, Katherine still talking.

"What did you say again? You're somebody's sister?" She gestured for me to leave the suitcase on a card table in the foyer. It was a tiny apartment, with a back window looking out to a white brick wall where somebody had painted a bunch of tulips, pink tulips. A couch draped with the same leopard-skin material as Katherine's pants occupied most of the living room. There was an electric range and small refrigerator in the bedroom, I would later see, along with twin beds. "Cynthia's," I said, opening a dumbwaiter near the back window. "What's this?"

"It's what I throw my dirty clothes down and hope that they come up clean," she said. "They don't."

"Oh," I said, and sat down. I did not quite know what to do. I had that sinking feeling of the newly arrived.

"Poor Marion," Katherine said, sitting next to me. I noticed how her legs blended in with the couch.

"I'm all right," I said, crossing my own legs and pulling the hem of my dress over my knees. "I'm all right," I said again.

"Of course you are," Katherine said, curling up at the end of the couch and lighting a cigarette from a pack on the coffee table. "It's just you're confused," she said, blowing the smoke out and toward me. "For all you knew, I was Doris and this was New York City. Now you've got Katherine and a dump. Poor thing. But it doesn't matter. We'll have fun. You can be the new Doris, if you'd like. Do you have a place to stay?"

"To stay?" I said.

"Yes, darling, to stay." I think it was the first time I had ever heard anyone my age use the word darling.

"No," I said.

"Cigarette?" she said.

38

I shook my head.

"Well," she said. "You'll stay here. Until you get your feet wet. Or on the ground. I'll show you the ropes. It'll take a few days, but you'll be fine."

She smiled, stubbed the cigarette into an oyster shell, and stood up.

"I hope Doris is all right," I said, as she walked around to the back of the couch.

"God, Doris. Well who knows, really. It had something to do with a Bill or a John or the other one, Remington something. Can you imagine? Sounds like a king. Listen," she said, sitting on the arm of the couch. "Let's eat out. There's nothing here anyway, and we only have Sterno."

"All right," I said, not wanting to be rude, and so we did. That night and every night after, it seemed, usually with some unsuspecting date picking up the tab. Oh, I know what you'll say about that, but you have to understand these were different times. We were encouraged to be children and so we acted that way, one party after another, not a thought to think except who we might choose, at the end of what felt like one long collective evening, to spend the rest of our lives with.

Take, for instance, Doris. Katherine got a postcard from her not long after I moved in. She had flown to Miami impromptu, on the arm of some lawyer she once typed for, and had married him in what she called a "cathedral by the sea." Who knows where Doris is now. Anyway, we packed the few things she had left behind and mailed them to her. Katherine, who did adopt the name Kat, insisted we keep one or two of Doris's outfits. At that time, all the girls were about the same size, and Katherine believed it was only right, given what Doris had put us through. In truth, Doris had put me through absolutely nothing, but Katherine had a gift for persuasion. She had come to New York to become an actress, and every afternoon she took the subway downtown and stood in a large gymnasium with several hundred girls our age, practicing various exercises for the stage. She had signed up before she left Pennsylvania, putting close to fifty dollars down to join a team of working professionals who would help "shoot her to the stars."

"It's like shooting myself in the foot," she'd say, coming back to the apartment just as the sun went down on the Hudson. The weather had turned warmer, and we would walk to the base of the George Washington Bridge and have a drink in Riverside Park. We'd walk slowly, our hats shading our faces, our lipstick fresh. People were everywhere in the streets—sitting on stoops watching children playing stickball or jacks, listening to radios, their collapsible lawn chairs arranged in circles. It was the season when it feels as if the entire city empties its pockets outdoors. The park was beautiful and safe, and there were thousands of girls like us living in the neighborhood. We knew who we were: We rarely shopped for food. On our secretaries' salaries we bought handbags, instead, and pumps and bathing suits and stockings and scarves to knot around our throats.

Sometimes, at the foot of the George Washington Bridge, Katherine and I would try to count the number of cars coming into the city and the number of cars leaving, calculating whether the city was filling up or draining out. If it had been a bad day for us, we'd say the city was draining out, that it just couldn't keep all of us here any longer, that we had other places to go. If it had been a good day, we'd say it was filling up, that more and more carloads of men were crossing into it—back from the war in Korea, or about to head off to it, hair shoe-polish black, Tyrone Powers to our Lana Turners, coming to take us away, hah hah!

New York 1954

We laughed. Katherine did this very well. I couldn't imitate it for you, or the way she smiled, or the way she convinced me to wear eyeshadow and to pluck my eyebrows into what she called an eighth of the moon. She wore pedal pushers, even when we went to the park. She liked to link arms and promenade to the tennis courts on 120th, where the boys from Columbia batted balls across the net and hooted when they saw the Puerto Rican girls walk by.

That summer she got cast in a play downtown. She told me it was a lewd bourgeois romp, which, given my limited exposure to the theater at the time, I interpreted as a slightly darker version of *The Pajama Game*. I had been taken by some dates to Broadway once or twice, but mostly we went to the movies. I particularly remember one film. The boy I went with had red hair the color of mine, and we both sat mortified through *Bitter Rice*—do you know it? The actress, whose name has escaped me, shimmies through the paddies in a wet blouse and skirt up to here. I can picture her perfectly, one bare shoulder, mud on her face. When the lights went up, I felt my own face, half expecting it to singe my fingers. My date's blush went even deeper. I don't think I'd been that embarrassed since I announced to the five insurance men I typed for that it was so hot outside I might just have an orgasm. But you remember that story. I was just shy of twenty and had, quite truthfully, no idea what the word meant, or rather I thought I knew—I had read it in a book once and believed it had something to do with a flush. When the rest of them laughed, Happy chided them, saying that I didn't know what I was talking about.

"I most certainly do," I said, and promptly left the room.

But now I've gotten ahead of myself. I have already told you that I lied to get that job as one of the secretaries to those men, that I wrote on my application I spoke six languages and had a master's degree in history. It didn't seem to have made much difference; four of the five insurance men asked me to dinner before my first month was out. I imagine they found me amusing. Well I was, actually, to all of them except Happy. No one was expected to be entirely aboveboard. Girls like us were inventing new lives, playing a game before our married lives began. I know you won't approve of this, but this is simply how it was.

Anyway, on the day of Katherine's opening night, I decided to take a long lunch break and find her a dozen roses. I had my heart set on buying bright yellow roses and had a vision of myself presenting them to her on stage. As I have said, I had no real idea what the play was about. The little I knew of Katherine's role was that it required her to faint, because she had been practicing for weeks on the leopard-skin couch, pulling the coffee table out of the way so she could stand square, facing the front door, muttering something, then collapsing straight back. I watched from my place at the card table. I had taken up smoking and would sit, my cigarette burning in its oyster shell, my eyes narrowed, ready to critique her performance. I remember repeating the word "grace" a lot, and "poise"—words from the women's magazines that were becoming popular at the time. You'd see girls like us reading them on the subway downtown, our hands in fresh white gloves.

Anyway, yellow roses were considerably exotic and couldn't be purchased just anywhere. The insurance office was in midtown, but I hadn't been at the job more than a few months and had no idea where to go. Unfortunately, the only person around to ask was Happy—the others had taken one of the clients to the Yale Club—and so I mustered the courage and knocked on his office door. I say unfortunately because he was the least friendly of the five, and though he had come to my defense after the orgasm gaffe he had barely acknowledged my presence since. None of the other secretaries knew much about him, except that he had remained in France for several years after the war, which he referred to as his tenure with *der Führer*, and that he walked with a cane as a result of the injuries he got in North Africa. He was what we called dashing, with a mustache thin as an ink line and the most delicate hands, long fingers with nails bitten to the quick. I imagine his nickname was meant to be ironic; he rarely smiled, and when he did, it looked like a grimace.

I found him sitting on the edge of his desk. I noticed he wore argyle socks (of course I was looking down), and for some reason, I was immediately drawn to the narrowness of his feet. I had knocked, and he had said come in, and when I finally got the nerve to look directly at him I saw that he had not even bothered to look up, that he remained entirely engaged in a newspaper crossword puzzle. He had removed his suit jacket, and his bright white short, buttoned at the cuffs, seemed too large for him.

I stood there for a moment, waiting. I had never been in his office alone. Mostly I took dictation in the conference room, a sunnier place with windows, where the insurance men met every morning at ten and for lunch. I believe I coughed. Can you picture me? Katherine had me in A-line skirts and short waist jackets. I had a pack of cigarettes in my purse and bright red lipstick. I wore what Katherine called Doris's scent. She said it had worked for Doris and my intentions were undoubtedly similar. I can't remember the name of it, though it had violet in the title; on occasions, when I overdid it, Katherine would call me her stinking violet.

Happy continued to stare at the crossword puzzle. "I need an eight-letter word for—," he finally said.

My mind immediately buzzed. This is what it has always done when I am asked a question I can't answer.

"No idea," I said.

It was then that he looked up. Perhaps he had thought I was someone else; he seemed surprised to find me in front of him and he stood, awkwardly, as if I had caught him ironing in his underwear. I wasn't sure why he appeared so embarrassed, but my own terrible shyness plowed under any curiosity.

"I'm sorry," I said. I tend to apologize in these situations. "I'm looking for yellow roses."

He looked around the office.

"Plumb out," he said.

"For a friend. My roommate. Katherine. Well, she's Kat now, actually, but the point is, she's an actress and this is her first big part and I wanted to find her yellow roses. The lucky kind." I repeat my words here only to show you how bumbly I was; quite truthfully, in those days you weren't used to being alone in a room with a man without his suit jacket on who had a way of looking at you as if he knew full well you spoke only one language, and that not too terribly gracefully. He lit a cigarette and offered me one. I declined. To smoke in front of your boss was worse than brushing your hair in a diner.

He appeared to be thinking and so I waited, and after a moment he stubbed his cigarette in a well-used ashtray and told me he would show me, that he needed the air. We took the elevator down together, saying nothing.

It must have been one of the hottest days on record in Manhattan, although the heat didn't seem to bother him. He grew more and more animated as we weaved our way to the florist, telling funny stories about trying to distinguish Nazis from Frenchmen after the war, and how there was little difference, and how, on the ship back from Europe not so many years earlier, they had had one particular moon-filled night where the flotsam collided with the jetsam and the flotilla had to be sunk. I had no idea what he was talking about, of course. I had dated a few boys who had been in the Second World War, though they were a bit old for me. Those boys didn't say much about it, and when they did I changed the subject. I have never liked the sound of boys' voices talking about war, though Happy's was somehow different, lighter, empty. It made me think of a giant iridescent soap bubble, and I felt as if I could float on his voice, ride that bubble high over Manhattan; it was that kind of afternoon.

When we reached the florist shop, Happy propped the door open for me with his cane and bowed as I went in. It was a touchingly senti- mental gesture, one I am reminded of to this day whenever a stranger holds the door. Inside, the florist told us he had yellow fresia and yellow glads, but no yellow roses. We stood in front of the refrigerator for a long time, pretending to consider iris and Shasta daisies, liking the cold, before the florist stepped in and asked us to please make our selection.

"Fresia," I said.

"That's it!" Happy said.

"What?"

"The eight-letter word for—"

I counted on my fingers.

"But fresia only has six letters," I said.

Happy looked at me for a long moment. "Almost perfect," he said, which at the time I didn't understand.

▼

Happy insisted on carrying the white box of fresia back to the office. It was difficult for him to maneuver both it and his cane, but he seemed determined and so I let him. I remember passing Saint Patrick's Cathedral. There was some sort of ceremony going on, a wedding or a baptism, and we stopped and watched the families pose on the great stone steps, waiting for the photographer to give them a signal.

When we got back, I put the box of fresia in the office refrigerator and went to my desk. There were several hours of dictation I had neglected in the morning, and so I put on my earphones and pressed the foot pedal, starting the dictaphone tape. I heard Mr. Springborn's voice and began to type. It must have been some time before I noticed Happy standing in front of me.

"Yes?" I said, removing the earphones.

"Your friend's play," he said. He shifted to his good leg. "Do you think it might be something I'd enjoy?"

We met downtown at a restaurant he had suggested. He offered to pick me up, but I said no. With your father, I would never have considered anything else, but with Happy the rules seemed absurd. Have I told you he was handsome? Conventionally, yes; I believe he had blue eyes. But not handsome in the way of your father or the other boys I dated at the time. They had a kind of freshness, a hopefulness to them that was then quite common, round cheeks and dimpled chins—men you could more easily picture running on playgrounds in long shorts than working in banks, or on Wall Street. Perhaps from the years he spent sorting Nazis from civilians in Paris, or from God knows what that I never found out, Happy had, well, Katherine later called it gravitas, a word I had never before heard. To me, he simply had the good looks and mystery of a certain kind of stranger, one you might glimpse from a train as he waited on the platform for someone entirely unlike you—someone older, perhaps, with an illegitimate child or a talent for poetry. He was a poem. That's better. The kind of poem you read in a book you have no intention of buying, one you have stumbled upon at the antiques shop, where you've been looking for stained glass, or salt and pepper shakers.

But I've strayed from the point. The point is, when I walked into the restaurant I believed I might be that woman he would have waited for, at least at that instant, entering, dressed to the nines in my Anne Fogarty and Capezios, a hat of some sort pinned with an amber stickpin of Doris's and her violet perfume in full bloom. Happy spotted me and stood in the way men used to do, and I felt, quite truthfully, that heady love you could feel only in those days, that terrible height. Too high, perhaps. There was something about the look of him, the way he nervously pulled out my chair, rearranged the bread in the bread basket. I sat and made small talk, trying to picture Happy meeting your grandfather, knowing he never would, understanding somehow that the all of it—the restaurant, the night, Katherine, Happy—would be only stories in my life, not my life. And as I dipped into my soup I felt that peculiar form of sadness one sometimes feels just on the other side of happiness.

I don't need to tell you that the play was a disaster. What else could it have been? It took place in a basement room of a jazz club called the Slippery Cave, and every once in a while, during the performance, the drummer upstairs would embark on a solo and drown out the actors' words entirely. This didn't matter, really. It was better not to hear them. Happy and I sat in the front row, I with my box of fresia in my lap, he with his cane. Katherine wore a kind of red gown and looked to me not unlike that actress in *Bitter Rice,* her hair tangled as if she'd run through several wind tunnels before arriving on stage. I remember a bearded older man circling her, prolonging the kill, and a particularly plush, red velvet divan, plump in the center of the stage onto which Katherine repeatedly fainted—with grace, I should add, blending in the way she had to our couch the day I arrived, leopard skin on leopard skin.

There were a handful of people in the audience, mostly friends of the actors, it seemed, and a few of the patrons from upstairs who wanted a break from the noise. Katherine shouted some sort of soliloquy at the end, something that sounded vaguely familiar before I realized I had heard bits and pieces of it from the shower for weeks. She looked beautiful when she stood beneath the light, the dustiness of the Cave stage sparkling around her, her eyeshadow a vivid, chameleon green. There were other actresses with minor roles, but Katherine was clearly the star. And only after she finished the soliloquy and collapsed on the divan again did I understand that this, truly, was the point.

Certainly not to Happy. He stood, applauding, and when the houselights came up I saw that he held his cane in the crook of his arm and had tears in his eyes. We walked around to meet Katherine at the makeshift stage door, and I presented her with the fresia, which had gotten a bit droopy during the performance. She stuck them in a beer mug and filled it with water, then left them on the stage, so, she said, they could be enjoyed by the custodians. I would have preferred she carried them home. That would have been, I thought, the polite thing to do, but she seemed to have forgotten about them as soon as she opened them, and when we left the Slippery Cave I could only imagine the custodians mistaking them for dead things and dropping them into the trash.

Once outside, Katherine linked one arm in mine and the other in Happy's. He seemed willing to lean on her rather than his cane, and we walked this way up Bleecker. I had never been to Greenwich Village before. It seemed there were girls like us everywhere and men with short beards and the sounds of saxophones from open windows. The night felt as hot as the day, and I ruined my Capezios on melted gum and the sticky residue of ice cream cones. But that didn't matter. We found ourselves in Washington Square Park and sat, the three of us, on a bench. Happy wanted to know everything about Katherine's role, and she told him, I remember, that she lived the words, she didn't say them, which seemed to be the right answer, and that, in truth, she had no idea whether the playwright, whom she had met during an earlier rehearsal but who had announced that he couldn't bear opening nights, had any true idea what he had written. She said he mentioned something about the sanctity of a sentence, which Happy again nodded to, but Katherine added that she felt too much sanctity got sanctimonious, didn't he agree? Frankly, for her, she said, it was all about the gown.

"It's not easy wearing red," she said.

"Is that right?" Happy asked. I was between them, and he had to lean forward a bit to look at her. I noticed that, in repose, his bad foot turned out, and I wondered if the rumor that he had shot off his own toe was based on truth.

"To wear red, you need a certain something," Katherine said. "I'll call it gravitas."

"Gravitas," Happy said, leaning back against the bench. "An eight-letter word."

Happy insisted on accompanying us home in a taxi, one of those big roomy ones you don't find anymore. It was a long way, and the cabbie took the outer drive, so that from where we were we could look straight at the buildings that formed the western edge of the city. We hardly said a word. I have always thought that from that angle Manhattan looks like one of those gems you find in hobby shops, something hard that's been cranked in two, its jaggedness polished to a point of value. It felt like family then, the three of us. Family I had never known before, or since. Oh, you and your father are family, of course; but there was something in that taxi, in that night, in the lights of the passing apartment buildings glowing the yellow of roses difficult to find anywhere else, fresia. Behind the brick walls, still warm with the day's heat, lives were forged among strangers with a tune and precision as sharp as some kind of elaborate mechanical clock. I wanted to put my arms around the all of it, but my arms would never reach. It was one of those evenings when you might kiss someone on the street corner simply because he walks a small white dog on a slender leash. I hope you will know what I mean by that.

Katherine rolled down her window and the warm air blew against our faces. If I had shut my eyes, I could have driven from there into forever. But I kept them open, and when the cabbie slowed down to look for the number of our building, I was the one who said "there" and pointed.

▼

Katherine and Happy stayed on the sidewalk for a while, talking. I went up and rolled down my stockings, brushed my teeth. I pulled back my covers and debated whether to turn off the light in our bedroom, knowing Katherine would have to find her way through the dark. I sat propped against the pillows and smoked a cigarette, trying to stay awake until she came in. The sheets felt cool. In those days, you didn't have air conditioners, and since there was no window in the bedroom a fan seemed pointless. Finally I stubbed out my cigarette and turned off the light. I lay there in the dark, my eyes open. Katherine came in some time later. She whispered my name to test if I were asleep, and I didn't respond. She tiptoed across the room and undressed, then she got into bed. I heard her cough a couple of times, roll one way or the other. Katherine was generally a heavy sleeper, so it seemed clear that she had every intention of refusing sleep until she had succeeded in waking me. I heard her whisper my name again, louder, and debated whether to keep pretending.

"What?" I finally said. It came out more harshly than I had intended.

"Do you like him?"

"Who?" I said.

"Who?" she said. "Don't be an idiot, darling. Happy."

"Him?" I said.

"Jesus Christ," she said. "Who else?"

I know she wanted me to turn on the light, to sit up in bed so we could talk. I did not. I let the dark press down on me like another layer of heat and felt the tears well in my eyes. Of course my feelings were hurt that Happy so clearly preferred Katherine, but that wasn't entirely it. Even then, I was aware that I had no real interest in him. Quite truthfully, he wasn't my type. But still, lying there in that window-less bedroom, in an apartment barely the size of your father's and my master bath, it was as if I could suddenly see my whole life open up in front of me, read my hand, so to speak, know that I would soon willingly, stupidly, surrender this freedom. And so I allowed myself to cry, and for a long time I refused to answer her.

Soon after that evening I met your father. We had three dates before he proposed. I said yes, immediately. He looked like Tyrone Power. It was the beginning of fall when I moved out, packing everything I had come with back into the hard plastic suitcase I had first lugged up those stairs. Katherine watched me make a final check from the leopard-skin couch.

"Guten Glück," she said. I turned to her. She had been cast as a German countess in a play she performed on Sunday nights in the basement of the synagogue down the street. On the weekends, she would run lines with Happy, who coached her on what he called her hangdog accent. He sat across from her now, his loafers— propped on the coffee table—speckled with paint. He had just that morning changed the pink tulips on the white brick wall to a fall montage. Now, when you looked out the window, it seemed as if somewhere above us a great wind shook the leaves from a maple.

"Oh dear," Katherine said. She stood and hugged me hard. Then she pulled away. "What am I going to do? *Ich bin sehr...*" she turned to Happy. "*Müde?*"

"*Nein,* not tired, darling," Happy said. "Sad."

"*Ja,*" she said. "I'm sad."

Your father coughed at that point, I believe. He had been waiting near the door. In those days, you rarely invited a boy upstairs, and I am sure he felt awkward standing in what had once been my apartment, among my things. I said another hurried goodbye as he lifted my suitcase. I can't remember whether Katherine and I hugged again, or whether I simply followed your father out the door. Either way, as I was leaving, Katherine stood waving at the top of the stairs. I remember how I returned her wave as I went down, turning back every few steps as if I were a passenger on a ship pulling out of a harbor, still looking long after what I was leaving had disappeared completely from my sight.

Tokyo

1963

Marion drinks her drink, watching the silhouette of her Japanese maid on the paper wall. Ice rattles as Marion lifts the glass to her lips, as the silhouette of her Japanese maid stands at the sink and then slowly turns toward the table.

Marion has found her Japanese maid through an advertisement in the English newspaper. I am hungry, the advertisement read.

The Japanese driver slams the trunk shut, the American husband waiting beside him to carry in the things he has brought from downtown. Next door, a boy wades buck naked through the snow, his hair a half-moon black, his mother watching from the window. She bows her head as the American husband passes, but he does not see her. He is looking at his wife, who stands in the doorway waiting. "I'm starving," he calls to her. "Chicken?"

Rebecca sings alone in her bed, the shadowy flames cast by the onionskin lantern flickering over her paper walls. She is very small, Rebecca; five years old. She has misbehaved and will not see what her father has brought her until tomorrow morning. There are rules to be maintained, Marion told her earlier. No matter what language.

The Japanese maid brings drinks to the Americans, her silhouette spreading like a watery drop of ink over the sliding paper wall that divides the kitchen from the living room. Next door, the boy squats in boiled snow, picking out the leaves and twigs and insect parts that float on the water's oily surface, lining them evenly on the rim of the wooden tub. Behind him, his mother kneels, scrubbing his small hard back with a sponge.

Marion and Robert sit with their legs pretzel-folded at the low dining room table, waiting for the Japanese maid to finish slicing the chicken meat from the bone.

"Doesn't she have pretty little hands?" Marion says. "I wish I had pretty little hands. Look. Look at my big ugly hands."

Robert does not look at Marion's hands; he looks at the line that parts the Japanese maid's hair, the skin like a white crack dividing a black egg.

"Today," Marion says, "I found something remarkable. Something from the emperor's collection, I am convinced. A gourd. Six chrysanthemum leaves stamped on its underside. I read somewhere that's the emperor's insignia. Have you heard that?"

Robert nods, looking past Marion to where the Japanese maid slides the paper wall back on its track, her silhouette shrinking as she moves into her room behind the kitchen.

"Apparently, the emperor loved chrysanthemums," she continues. "Grew them or something. God, chrysanthemums."

"I can't even think of what a chrysanthemum looks like," Robert says, turning toward her. "What does it look like, anyway?"

"God, chrysanthemums—I don't know. Like a marigold, I guess. They smell terrible."

Robert picks the wishbone off his plate, twirls it in his fingers.

"Look," he says. "A wish."

"For what?" she says.

"I don't know." He looks from the greasy stem to Marion's face. "For pretty little hands?"

In the room on the other side of the kitchen, the Japanese maid sits on an American Army cot reading Onenesses, while next door the boy's mother scrubs too hard. The boy turns and slaps her cheek; on her white skin blooms a small red handprint.

The paper wall slides back so suddenly that the Japanese maid drops the Onenesses to her lap. "Shhhhhh," Robert says, pressing his fingers to his lips. He looks down at her; he has never been in the room before and is unsure what he intends to do now. There is a longing about him to stand in an unfamiliar place. So he does. It's as simple as that. He stands and looks, although most of the things he cannot see: the photograph of the Japanese maid and her dead family slid into the small space between the mirror glass and its frame, the ivory-handled hairbrush the Japanese maid uses to brush Rebecca's hair, the hard-boiled eggs she has stolen from the kitchen to take to a friend she visits on Thursdays, when Marion shops at the grocery story for westerners and cooks their meals by herself. "Thank you," he says. "May I sit down?"

The Japanese maid nods, and Robert sits next to her. He cannot think of what to say. "Do you know what our emperor loves?" he says after a time. But the Japanese maid keeps her head bowed, her small powdered feet tucked beneath her. She does not understand a word of English.

"It's not only the Koreans they despise," Marion says, shaking vinegar onto the cold rice, then scooping it up in a torn piece of seaweed. "They think everybody else is a barbarian. It's in their Bible or something."

Robert sips his tea.

"You should see how she treats the milkman. He's Vietnamese, I think."

Rebecca passes her parents walking straight and quick into the kitchen, where the Japanese maid's movements have stilled at the window. Robert watches as the Japanese maid turns, as his daughter slides the paper wall back on its track.

"God knows what they talk about," Marion says.

Next door, the boy urinates in the snow, one small hand guiding his penis—the stream of urine reflecting the sun, steaming in the cold.

Rebecca sits at the kitchen table watching the Japanese maid scale fish. Fish scales stick to her cheeks, her eyelashes. She picks them off and presses them to her wrist, to the soft skin there, where they stay; she thinks she could swim deep underwater, where the Japanese maid has told her little girls sometimes go to be other things and to see what they are missing.

Rebecca knows what she is missing. Birthday parties. She hasn't been to a birthday party. And she has no brothers or sisters, she says. None. The Japanese maid listens, peeling radishes and looking out the window to where the exterminators pick peach beetles off the peach trees and place them carefully into the snow.

In the market, Marion argues. She is cold and stamps her feet. In her hands is a wooden doll—a wish doll, the Korean market seller has told her, with one wish left. The doll is small and round, painted red. One eye has been crossed through with a black "x", the other remains a blank oval.

"Special for you, Jackie Kennedy," says the Korean man. "Good price."

"Too much," Marion says.

"Special for you, Miss America. Good price. Good wish."

Later, the boy stands naked, his fingers gripping the smooth wooden sill of a window into the American house. He stands on his tiptoes, watching as the American woman naps, her head pointing north with the dead. Bad luck. He sees the clean wishbone on the wooden sill and takes it with a quick child motion, turning and running to where his mother stands waiting. When he reaches her, he burrows into the place where she has loosely tied her kimono, pushing his lips to one of her flattened breasts, its dark nipple. His small white teeth bite down. He sucks hard.

In the almost dark of the late winter afternoon, the Japanese driver slams the trunk. Beside him, Robert waits, ready to carry in the rust-red chrysanthemum he has bought downtown, its tiny buds not yet opened, its leaves a dark green, almost black.

Next door, the boy sleeps in his mother's arms. On his cheek, an eyelash—fragile as a crack on marble—has drifted.

Robert carries the chrysanthemum to Marion, who waits in the doorway.

"What a color!" she says.

Robert goose-steps through the snow. "The emperor marches home from a long day at the office," he says. "He has won every battle."

"Oh darling," says Marion, taking the plant from his hands and kissing his cold lips. "My hero."

"Why does their chicken always taste like fish?" Marion says.

"It tastes all right to me," Robert says.

"Would someone please talk to her? Would someone please ask her why their chicken always tastes like fish?" Marion says, louder. Rebecca looks down, then shoves away from the table and leaves the dining room.

"Now what?" Robert says to Marion.

"Now what, what?" she says.

Far away, swallows drink from the river, their twin shadows ascending into one as they rise, startled by the Japanese driver who crosses the bridge on foot. Near him, on the far bank of the river, an old woman sits, her silhouette quivering on the slow river water.

Tokyo 1963

"Before Manchuria," the Japanese driver calls to her. "I owned a bicycle."

Rebecca is sent to bed, the oilskin lantern casting cats, pigs, chickens, and dogs from her hand as she sings to herself.

Underneath her pillow is the photograph of the Japanese maid's dead family. There are four of them: the Japanese maid, her Japanese husband, and two sons. The boys look like twins, though they are simply close in age. They wear hats like upside-down bowls, and their cheeks are bright with winter. The Japanese husband stands behind them, a hand on each boy's right shoulder. The Japanese maid does not look like a maid. She wears a yellow dress and holds a yellow pocketbook, the kind Rebecca would like for her birthday, the kind she will wish for and receive, carrying until she turns ten, when another pocketbook will take its place and the yellow one will be stored, its silky lining stained with pen ink, in a box kept in the attic marked *Japan things*.

But for now, she knows none of it, she only wants, while down the hall in the darkened room her mother sits, ice rattling as she drinks her drink, as she watches Robert's silhouette on the paper wall. He works at his desk, unaware of Marion's watching, growing gigantic with the waning light. Soon he will seep onto her, over her, and she will be blanketed, the small wooden doll in her lap staring up, its wishing eye fixed.

Rochester

1965

Today I've been watching it snow and thinking of Dorothy. This was in Rochester, before your sister was born, when you were six or seven and your father worked most weekends. (I have always thought it ironic that your father made our living as an efficiency expert, a job that required so many hours of overtime.) We lived in a pink brick Georgian at the end of a cul-de-sac called Country Club Road. Your father had flown out from Detroit to find it and had bought it over one weekend. You were too young to travel at the time, so we stayed behind. I remember he called from the Holiday Inn to let me know he had found a house and how, when I asked him to describe it, he said it had an "expansive den."

We moved the following weekend, and I suddenly found myself in a pink Georgian in the middle of a Rochester winter. I tried to keep my spirits up. I went around to some of the homes where snowmen had been built, ostensibly looking for playmates for you. Dorothy lived in one of those grand cold Tudors with leaded windows and azaleas and box hedges trimmed into spades. Her Christmas decorations were still out—garlands of evergreen wrapped with white lights and a red-ribboned wreath on the front door. I rang the doorbell, and Dorothy opened the door as if she were expecting me.

"You're here," she said.

"Marion Clark," I said, holding out my hand.

"Oh," she said, shaking it. "I'm sorry."

"You thought I was someone else?"

She nodded. "Forgive me, it's cold. Come in."

She was a woman who could say "forgive me" without batting an eye.

The inside of her house felt nothing like the outside; it held a sweet thick smell I recognized as incense. There were large pillows scattered around the floor in the living room and plants whose tendrils grew up and over the windows. I accepted her offer of a drink, though it was two o'clock in the afternoon, and, for those years at least, your father and I had a rule about no cocktails before six.

I asked for an old fashioned. It sounded right. She nodded when I said it, as if I had passed a secret test; then she led me into the living room. "You *are* who I was waiting for," she said, ducking out. I sat on the couch. It was draped with a batik fabric that had hundreds of tiny mirrors stitched into it, and I remember how I thought that if light ever got through those heavy webbed-green windows the mirrors would reflect it like so many diamonds and the couch would appear afire.

Dorothy returned with an ornate tray and sat down across from me on one of the floor pillows. "So," she said, handing me my drink. "Let me guess. You're new. You're bored. You're looking for playmates for your child but you're really looking for company."

"I guess you could say that," I said.

"Well, cheers then," she said, lifting her glass. "To playmates."

"Salut," I said, wanting to sound continental. I felt paltry in comparison to this creature in black silk. I had worn my usual wool slacks and snow boots. How could I have known?

I sipped my drink. She had made it quite strong, and from the first taste I felt transported.

"So," she said. "Let me tell you what there is to know. First off, I'm Dorothy. I don't think I ever said that. Not Dot or Dottie, please, but Dorothy. My mother was very particular about this. Anyone who would call me anything but got a talking down to, including teachers and boyfriends. She named me Dorothy after Dorothy Lamour, who I have later come to find out goes by Dot. But mother's dead, so there you have it. Second, I live in this monstrous house with a husband, Rick, and twin sons, Richard and Ross. It was not my idea to go with 'R,' but Rick insisted so what could I do. I had just been through forty-eight hours of labor and, besides, he's from Canada of all places." Dorothy paused and took a sip of her drink. Behind her, through the thick glass, I saw that it had begun to snow, again, and wondered if she wasn't cold in nothing more than silk.

"We moved here about seventeen months ago and the boys think it's great and Rick plays golf and I am bored out of my mind. Rochester, for God's sake. Who would have thought I would end up here? I am the daughter of missionaries. I grew up everywhere, including Calcutta and Peking, and I am the first to tell you that life is elsewhere." She took a deeper sip. "Do you know what I mean?"

"I suppose so," I said. I felt hot in my coat, but she hadn't offered to take it. It was as if I had entered some sort of circus fun house, and Dorothy sat before me as the reflection of what I could become, if I squinted my eyes, if I poured a drink at two o'clock and burned incense in Rochester.

"Oh, I'm not saying there's nothing to do here. There's the club and a good bridge group and dances every Saturday and around Christmas they have the Bachelors' Ball, which is really for all the married folk who go and get blasted to the hilt and switch husbands and that sort. We'll talk about that into the next year and the spring, and it will give us something to think about come fall, again, when we are feeling kind of blowzy and old, and when we unpack the ornaments and find two shattered, again. Too bad you weren't moved in before that, you could have met the gang and added your own rumor to the mill."

I must say it got to a point where I simply watched her mouth move. I could not get past a woman using the word "blowzy" in a sentence and getting away with it. She sounded so grand. She reminded me of a lone exotic fish, the type you might see in one of those over-priced pet stores swimming around and around and around the aquar-ium, the glass sides of which are almost opaque with the mossy green of algae, as if the poor thing has been forgotten.

"Come on," she said at last, draining her drink. "The boys won't be home for an hour, and I need to shop. You come. I want help."

I stood. I'm not sure how much time had passed, but I remember thinking that you would be fine, set with the new baby-sitter. Dorothy walked to the hall closet and put on a very full raccoon coat. Then she opened the front door and stepped out. I followed her around to the garage.

"Don't you need the air?" she said, lighting a cigarette. She stood by the back garage door and smoked. "Rick doesn't let me do this in the house, and who can blame him, the plants and all. Terrible habit, really. My teeth are yellow. But it gives me something to do, don't you think that? If nothing else, this is something to do." We shared the cigarette, then stamped into the garage and got into her car, a type of which I cannot remember. She was not a woman who would take much stock in automobiles, though she did love clothes and had the most elegant wardrobe of anyone I had ever known, before or since. I remember when I got the news that she was dead, my second or third thought was of those clothes, of what they would have chosen to put her in for her burial.

We drove into downtown Rochester fast, through yellow lights just changed to red. She had turned on the radio, and it felt wonderful to have had one drink and to be riding in the front seat of a warm car in the middle of an afternoon with a new friend. She pulled over when we got to the department store—one of those once-grand chains you find in depressed cities. I felt a bit blue stepping out of the car into the cold to enter such a faded place. We should have pulled up to Bonwit's and left the keys for the valet. But soon the mood shifted; there were aisles of brightly lit things and a makeup counter where a few well-preserved women stood in lab coats and beckoned us closer. I was game, but Dorothy took my hand.

"Come on," she said, and led me to the wooden escalator. We rode up to the sportswear section on the second floor.

"What are we looking for?" I asked.

"You'll see," she said, and smiled.

She led me past sportswear toward the back of the second floor, through a maze of girdled mannequins and mounds of flesh-colored bras and panties. The nightgowns hung along the back wall, a rack of silky expensive things I would have normally passed right by. Dorothy stood in front of them. "Aren't they divine?" she said.

They were part of some kind of early Easter display—pink and blue and green and yellow silks. "I can't wear yellow, but you," Dorothy said, choosing a yellow one from the rack, "you could do it."

She held the yellow nightgown up to me and admired it. I looked back at her, again thinking of her as some kind of mirror in which I stood reflected. "It's lovely," I said.

Dorothy smiled. "But you do like it?" she said. I took the hanger from her and carried the nightgown over to the real mirror. It was difficult to tell whether I liked it or not. I felt foolish. I held the yellow silk nightgown over my wool coat and wool slacks, sure that if I actually tried it on I would look absurd, with my thick socks and pale arms.

"It's lovely, really," I said, carrying it back to Dorothy and putting it on the rack. "Perhaps I'll come back for the sales."

Dorothy shrugged. "I think it's a wonderful color for you. Not many can wear yellow," she said.

She stood and stared at me for a moment. I attributed the strangeness I felt to the old fashioned.

She invited me in as we pulled up to her garage, and I accepted. I had so rarely had company in the afternoons in Detroit. Once inside, she offered another drink. There was something of a party about that day—a new friend, a spontaneous shopping trip, two old fashioneds before six. I felt as if the world could indeed open up for me, and I could step in.

She brought out the fresh drinks on a new, even more ornate tray. I pulled off my snow boots, and when she offered to take my coat I said yes. I felt so comfortable, as if I could curl up on the mirrored couch and sleep for years. I tried to explain the day to your father that night, but I could not find the right words.

With Dorothy, the right words were easy. I told her about our moves, and about you and your birth. I told her how your father and I hoped to have another child.

She told me again how the "R" names had been her husband's idea. She told me again that her parents were missionaries and that the white porcelain elephant in the corner had come directly from Burma, before they had shut the gates, and that her mother had been a great beauty with blonde hair and that everywhere they had gone the people in the villages had been far more interested in looking at her hair than they had been in hearing her preach about God and Jesus.

Then she asked me did I believe in God and Jesus, and at the time I did, so I said yes.

She said there were plenty of churches she could show me, but that she could not go inside. That she had sworn off it like she had sworn off any more children and any more sex with her husband.

It was at that point I said I should go, not because I disliked her using such an unfamiliar word, but because I knew that with Dorothy I could say what I might regret, that I could speak words that had been, before this, light as balloons drifting through my mind. To speak them would be to give them heft and weight.

"Goodbye, love," she said at the door, kissing me on both cheeks. "See you tomorrow?"

"Of course," I said.

She held my coat up for me, and I put my arms through the sleeves and felt so entirely warm, from her, from this, from the promise of another day, that I walked home slowly through the bitter cold, balancing on the ridged rain gutters that ran on either side of Country Club Road, slipping some on the ice. It was that part of the day I would later come to know as the blue hour. Dorothy said she had picked it up somewhere, she thought perhaps Paris. L'heure bleue. She said it seemed to her always the best way to describe that time of early evening when the world seemed trapped in melancholy, and all its regrets for all its mislaid plans for the day were spelled in the fading clouds.

This is, quite truthfully, how she would phrase things.

Once home, I picked you up and kissed you, and the two of us drove the baby-sitter back to wherever she had come from. On our way home, we stopped for something at the store. Running in, I reached into my coat pocket for my wallet and felt the silk, wadded down so deep that I thought for an instant I had never noticed the fine lining of the wool. Then I pulled it out. The yellow nightgown, of course. To this day I am not sure whether Dorothy stole it for me, or whether she simply paid, slipped it out of its bag, and put it in my pocket. I am sorry that I felt too shy to ask her. I have always harbored suspicions.

Dorothy died several years after we moved to Norfolk. I got the news over the telephone. We had lost touch, but that was not so unusual when a woman stayed in a place only until her husband's next transfer. She had sent me Christmas cards, of course, and a longer note when she heard about your sister's birth.

When Rick called, we were packing for Durham, getting things organized for the movers the next day. I had been feeling the nostalgia I have always felt before leaving. But it had been a bad place for us, Norfolk, and I believed that somehow we could begin again in North Carolina. When I hung up the phone, I went back to what I had been doing, rolling china into sheaves of newspaper, marking cardboard boxes *den, kitchen.* I did not think of Dorothy. Instead, I thought of the next neighborhood, the next house: how I would paint the living room walls, paper the bedrooms; how I would knock on the front doors of the houses on our new street, introducing myself, introducing you, accepting when the ones at home invited us in for tea and cookies. It felt somehow impossible to think of anything else, to think of the way she must have looked, so indiscreet, so inelegant, slumped against the steering wheel of that automobile going nowhere, idling in the garage over the long weekend Rick had chosen to take the boys camping. Instead, I pictured her in her coffin, pictured her in a yellow silk nightgown, because she always said things like silky nightgowns helped to chase away that blowzy feeling that came with every blue hour, when no man or beast, she said, should be left to swim alone.

Norfolk

1966

After the baby was born, Robert carried the things Marion had asked for in a bag to her room—a yellow nightgown from the bottom drawer of their bureau, clean underpants. He walked slowly, signing in at the front register and pinning the visitor's pass they gave him onto the lapel of his raincoat, passing the gift shop and cafeteria, reaching the elevator banks where, just beyond, he noticed the opened door of the chapel and saw, or believed he saw, a man his age kneeling, praying at the end of the center aisle between the pews, his hat beside him dark from rain.

"I'm sorry to be trouble," Marion said when he came in. Along the radiator, bouquets of arranged carnations and mums were evenly spaced; in the corner, helium balloons drooped between the ceiling and the floor.

"Not at all," he said.

She took the bag and looked. "You brought this one?" she said. "I thought I said the new one. This one won't fit. I thought I said yellow."

"It is yellow," he said.

"I meant *yellow* yellow. There's a newer one there."

The helium balloons dipped. A nurse wheeled in Marion's dinner on a tray, jockeying the tray around so that it fit neatly across Marion's waist.

Robert watched the nurse leaving, then walked to the window; the rain had not let up, and below, in Parking Lot C, people slammed their doors and ran fast into the hospital. He put his hand to the glass and thought of some story he had heard about a boy in a place like this. "Did you go?" Marion asked from behind him. "Did you see her?"

"For a few minutes," he said. A card stuck in one of the flower arrangements read: *Our Prayers with You.* "They didn't want me to stay."

The boy in the story had been flown up from Cuba, or Miami, and had wanted to see snow. Someone had driven to the foothills of the Alleghenies and packed a snowball in an ice chest, carrying it over the Virginia back roads. The boy had never been so close to snow as when the person who drove to the mountains returned and stood there with it, holding it up in the parking lot, yelling, the boy leaning out the window ready to catch, his hands reaching, his pajamas on, his feet bare, his dark eyes hot with fever, steady.

No. That couldn't be right, he thought. These windows don't open. The boy must have simply stood looking out the way he stands now, his hands pressed up on the glass.

From the parking lot, the boy would have appeared quite small.

M arion asked Robert to help her stand so she could go into the bathroom and brush her teeth. She had not worn this nightgown for years, she told him. Didn't it smell like Rebecca?

She hunched over the porcelain sink, her elbows on either side of it, balanced, and rubbed a circle of white cream around each eye. She looked out of place in this nightgown, a nightgown Robert knew now he had not seen her wear since Rebecca was born. Marion was smaller then, or perhaps the nightgown had shrunk. The sleeves bunched high on her wrists, and the shoulder seams pulled too close to her neck. In the nightgown, she looked like a different, younger Marion—a Marion he might have known years ago.

"I need a walk," she said. "Will you walk me, please?"

He blinked as he stepped with her into the brightly lit hospital hallway, the door slowly closing behind them. Marion moved awkwardly, pushing one foot in front of the other in the paper slippers they gave her when she first went into labor. Marion, he thought, holding her arm as tightly as he could. She was thirty-one years old; they were eleven years married in June. The first words she had ever said to him were "heads or tails?"

At times, after the baby was born, Robert put his wristwatch close to his ear to listen to the sound of seconds ticking.

After the baby was born, Robert told Rebecca he wanted to speak to her upstairs. She was sitting downstairs in the den, watching television. A cartoon rooster—much bigger than a rooster should be— leaned cross-legged against a doghouse, talking to the dog that sat inside.

Robert stood in the den doorway watching, then he took off his coat and walked upstairs, removing his jacket and his tie along the way.

"Now," he said. He had not intended his voice to sound so stern. When she appeared in their room, he softened it. "Sit here a minute, next to me," he said.

"My show is on," Rebecca said.

"Please," he said.

"What?" she said, climbing up on the bed, falling into him, then straightening up.

He could hear the television going downstairs.

"You have a sister," he said.

"Cool. What's her name?" Rebecca said.

He smoothed her hair. "We haven't decided. She's still in the hospital. Your mother's there with her. They don't let baby girls leave until they've grown some hair, and she's bald as a billiard ball."

"She is?" Rebecca said.

"Don't worry. They'll be in the hospital for a few more days. They'll be home in a few days," he said.

He sat on the edge of his bed next to his daughter, his hands in his lap, his hard office shoes on the shag rug they had ordered for the entire house.

"Can I watch the rest of my show now?" Rebecca said.

After the baby was born, the men from the company brought donations for the children's ward, cash and stuffed animals and whatever their wives got down from the attic. They piled the things at noon, their lunch hour, on one of the tables in the cafeteria, mildly talking of sports and company things: a chemical spill at the plant in Lamar, the newspapers reporting that chemicals had leaked into the Mississippi and a lot of money would have to be spent. Already, fish were belly up and bloated on the banks of the Sabine.

After the baby was born, Robert left Marion and returned home. Rebecca was elsewhere, taken by a neighbor for the night. Outside, the rain came down harder, matting the pine needles fallen in the woods that divided their house from the other houses in the neighborhood. Tree frogs clung to the underside of leaves. Weather he liked. Basement weather. There, he could listen to the rain in the gutters and play the radio low and pick up where he left off on the dollhouse. He was building a dollhouse for Rebecca's birthday. A surprise.

He walked into their bedroom as the telephone began to ring, the rings loud in what suddenly felt like an empty house. It was his friend, Jackson, who said he thought the office had collected a lot of loot; everyone sent their best; how was the baby?

"Up in the air," he lied, sounding foolish, as if someone had just asked him his plans for New Year's Eve.

"Ellie wants to speak to you," Jackson said.

"Robert?" Ellie said. "Robert? How's Marion?"

"Fine," he said.

"What can we do? Is there anything, do you need anything, has Marion got everything she needs there? How long will she be in? I've heard they—"

"Ellie," he heard Jackson say in the background.

"Thank you, Ellie, we're fine. Thank you."

"Let us know," Ellie said.

"Thank you, goodbye," he said.

"Goodbye," Ellie said.

He sat for a while. On the telephone stand a pair of Marion's earrings lay side by side.

After the baby was born, Babe Hutchinson, who played Bridge with Marion on Tuesdays, baked a lasagna for twenty. It was the least she could do, she thought, waiting for it to cool. She sat at her kitchen table and drank a cup of coffee, staring at the pattern of roosters and chickens covering her papered walls. The roosters looked startled, their eyes too bright a blue; it unnerved her, and she thought again of when she might strip the kitchen and get one of the nicer floral designs she had seen in some of her friends' powder rooms.

Upstairs she could hear the cleaning woman vacuuming.

"Well," she said, to nothing in particular; it was now about nine.

She finished her coffee and crossed the kitchen to the sink, rinsing the cup and putting it in the dishwasher. Then she wiped her hands and took a cigarette from the pack she kept on the windowsill, staring out the window at a suet ball her husband had hung on a bare branch of the hemlock. She lit the cigarette and crossed the kitchen again, reaching for the telephone mounted on the wall above the table. Over it, a laminated sheet listed the names of the women she generally spoke with each morning. The telephone had been mounted squarely on top of one of the roosters, a wedge of startled blue eye barely visible above the mounting screw.

Norfolk 1966

Eleanor Scarlet answered the phone as if she hadn't spoken a word all morning. Babe immediately knew, from the tone of Eleanor's voice, that Eleanor hadn't heard—and again, that small thrill, that elation Babe had felt since first learning last night, welled someplace within her.

After she hung up with Eleanor, Babe called the remaining women on the list: Joanie Aires, Gig Wentworth, Ann Spires, and Jane Thompson. Of the four, only Ann Spires had heard, since her husband played doubles Monday evenings with several men from the company.

Babe hung up the telephone and called to the cleaning woman that she would be going out; she crossed the kitchen to the counter where she had left the lasagna. Some tomato sauce had splattered on the floor in front of the stove. She took the sponge from the sink and squatted down to rub the stain out, wondering, as she always did, why she bothered to hire a cleaning woman at all.

As Babe worked the tomato sauce off her kitchen floor, Joanie Aires called Gig Wentworth.

"What's the likelihood?" Joanie wanted to know.

"Who could account for it?" Gig said.

The two let the telephone line cackle between them, each sitting alone at their kitchen tables. Joanie traced a blue-ink circle on a folded white napkin left from dinner the night before, stabbing at the circle several times with the point of her pen, then drawing a blue heart.

Both weighed the silence of the other.

"Well," Gig finally said.

Joanie absentmindedly shaded in the lower chambers of the heart, turning her sketch three-dimensional.

Gig cleared her throat. "Tell me," she said. "What do you think they do for something like that? I mean, have you heard of them doing anything?"

"Apparently this is not the first time it's happened, though it is extremely rare, I understand," Joanie said, repeating Babe's information. "Babe said she had seen some television program about it."

"Yes, I know, she told me," Gig said, straightening up some.

"Apparently you can put one in if you can find one, although I'm not sure how that's done," Joanie said. "What Babe said was that they had to find one exactly the same age, or weight, or something like that, since it would still be growing."

"How terrible," Gig said, wanting to sound better than she did. "Well, there but for the grace of God," she added, her voice pitched to a decidedly brighter tone.

After the baby was born, Robert walked to his study to sit and think. The lights in his study were low and green-glassed, the effect eerie in a night as dark as this one. He imagined that he looked like a painting of a man, a man whose wife had given him a book for his thirtieth birthday entitled, *If These Are the Best Years of My Life, Why Am I so Miserable?*, a man who ate one banana and a slice of dry toast every morning for breakfast. A man who once wore hats, but no longer.

Or perhaps he looked like a character from a book, a man sitting at his desk in his study, surrounded by mysteries. But in a book, there would be a knock on the study door. In a book, someone would eventually come in. Here, time passed and he remained alone.

He opened the top drawer of the desk and took a sheet of stationery from the stack there, smoothing it against the desktop. He planned to write Marion a letter, tell her a few things. More than once she had said she regretted they never corresponded this way. If she had loved him through a war or a European tour or during the nineteenth century it might have been so, she had told him. She might have saved his letters and passed them down to Rebecca. True love stories always begin with letters, she would say. Any great love you can think of.

Dear Marion, he wrote, then he crossed it out.

My dear Marion, he wrote.

Who would have imagined this would happen to us? This happens to other people, in other places, doesn't it? People you hear about—

He began again.

Dear Marion,

Rebecca said no one could get the rat's nest out of her hair but you, so you better come home soon to—

He began again.

Dear Marion,

Hello! I'm sitting—

He began again.

Dear Marion,

It is very late and I am tired.

He underlined the word "tired," the black ink blotting the stationery, an elegant ivory paper Marion had bought to write condolences and congratulations. Then he crossed out the word "tired" and began again.

After the baby was born, the ladies at the Club found a substitute for Marion and played their Tuesday game, sitting at the round table in the Clubhouse in front of the picture window facing the eighteenth hole, where men some years older than their husbands drove up the fairway, their small white balls plunking onto the bright-green green with softly audible thuds.

No one landed in the rough, as far as they could tell.

The bartender poured drinks—Manhattans—that the waitress carried to their table. It was a gorgeous day. The ladies lifted the small plastic-wrapped cracker packages from the bowl in the center of the table and tore them wide open with their teeth.

Jane Thompson arrived late.

"No word," she said, sitting down and gesturing to the waitress. She ordered a whiskey sour and picked up her hand.

"We're all having Manhattans," Gig Wentworth said.

"Of course," Babe Hutchinson said to Joanie Aires, "no one seems to have any new information. No one knows what to think. I mean, it's such an unusual thing."

Babe looked around the large Clubhouse table at the other women gathered. They smiled. Most were thinking of the crumbs in their laps, although Bambi Stevens, Marion's substitute, was thinking of her hand. She had never played so high on the ladder.

After the baby was born, Robert walked sock-footed to the kitchen wet bar and poured himself another bourbon. In this late night, he could hear the house shifting, settling. Outside, cicadas were as loud as a pulse in fear. June bugs clawed the screens, toads pissed in the rain gutters.

He pictured Marion sleeping in the hospital, her arms above her head; she looked like Rebecca, like his friends' wives; she looked nothing like the first day of her, of them, on the tennis court, her brown hair lightened red by sun, her legs tanned, her arms. Someone's friend.

He had approached her, too aware of his own thin legs. He had a feeling she would be someone he knew from the minute she spoke, someone he might have met before. He was a cadet. Tall. The day waned on the Hudson. It must have been nearly six.

She had looked at him and smiled, cocking her head in the way she still will when asking a question.

"Heads or tails?" she said.

"Heads," he said.

"You lose," she said.

"Robert Clark," he said, holding out his hand across the net.

"Marion Too-difficult-to-pronounce," she said.

The light seemed to follow her, as if she were a part of some once-grand garden: a piece of statuary brought in from Athens, or Rome, something carefully packed and guarded, some perfect lost form. After the game, she sat with her ankles crossed, her hands folded in her lap. Where had she learned that? She had slender fingers.

"My mother worked in a factory and my father was a union organizer and if anybody at this place knew I was Catholic I'd probably be tarred and feathered."

He didn't think so.

She said, "You cannot imagine. It is too much, the way people are."

She squinted, looked up at him. Her eyes were the green that lies beneath the surface of all things.

A few weeks later, they were married. Afterward, she had read him a poem written by a poet who was too much, too perfect. The poem he had always remembered, the poet he had forgotten: *If all*

the world and love were young, And truth in every shepherd's tongue,
These pretty pleasures might me move to live with thee and be thy
Love. It went on. He had forgotten.

He walked into the den and turned the television off. I have had
too much to drink, he thought. Entirely too much.

The rain had stopped, though water still dripped off the pines and
the heat Virginia traps in its red clay rose, fogging roads and fields—
the entire world an apparition that might disappear at the bend of a
road. Robert walked and smoked. On either side of him, houses were
set back from the road—each placed at the end of an asphalt drive,
each fortified with rhododendrons, magnolias, azaleas, forsythia, and
lawns of brittle crabgrass where mutts strained the ends of their chains,
locked to low magnolia limbs or stakes pounded into the red clay ground.

He did not need to see to know this neighborhood. He had lived in
this neighborhood before, in other places. The same towns, the same
names, the same roads. This one was bordered by a creek, a drainage
ditch, where daffodils first bloomed. Somewhere ahead, Marion had
planted a willow with Rebecca last Easter, the two of them returning
clay-stained, happy.

In the clearing fog, he could make out his own shadow, hatted, alone,
a pipe stuck between his clenched teeth, the bulb a small circle of black
turning his second self into a cartoon figure, a man hatted, alone, his
words inked out—a cartoon figure pursuing, or led by, a small empty
circle of speech. He would turn at Jackson's house, the two-story brick at
the end of the cul-de-sac.

He thought of ringing the bell. It pleased him. He thought of stealing up to Jackson's front door and pressing the small lit bell mounted on the door frame, of hearing the sound ringing through Jackson's house and knowing Jackson, asleep with Ellie, would wake suddenly, his heart pounding with the same fear he had felt waiting for the baby to be born, the feeling that something is not as it once was, the sense that something has moved out of place.

Robert drove into Parking Lot C, pulling into a parking space in the row closest to Marion's window. He turned off the car, the lights, and listened to the engine settle. He knew the workings of an engine; he had studied that before. He knew there were certain predictable things you could account for—soft brakes or carburetor rust—ways of recognizing the signs. Other parts broke down without warning.

Behind him, folded in a paper grocery bag, was the yellow nightgown. He had found it exactly where she had said it would be. His was such an easy task. Now he took it from the bag and opened the car door, stepping out.

Marion's window was as dark as her neighbors' windows, everyone apparently sleeping. For a time, he stood next to the car and willed her—willed her to turn on the light, to come to the window, to see him standing there below her. He might have held up the yellow nightgown and shouted her name, but it was too late and very dark. Who would hear him in the middle of this night, from this distance, in this place? Who would hear anyone at all?

A Place on a Lake

1966

After the baby was born, your father found a place for me in Virginia, a place on a lake. I can't remember the name of it, but that doesn't matter. The point is, it had once been a Boy or Girl Scouts' camp, and so the accommodations were quite rudimentary—scattered cabins set back from the lakeshore, four or five docks with canoes, one main cabin where we would gather three times a day for meals and where we would go, individually, to talk to the psychiatrist in residence. His name was Dr. Klein, and he had round spectacles, the kind you see now on architects and artists. His knee shook terribly, and, quite truthfully, his glasses and his rattling knee were about the strongest impressions he made on me. I remember he asked several questions about my relationship with you and your father, about how I felt the moment the baby was born, about why I did what I did afterward.

"What I remember best," I told him, "is how quiet the room was."

"What room?" he said.

"The delivery room," I said. I looked at him when I said it, not one to look away or to stretch out on the divan they had there for that purpose. "The place they took me." His spectacles flashed light. His knee jiggled his desk. Behind me, a window looked out to the slope of lawn down to the lakeshore. If I had turned around, I might have seen the other guests going about their days, swimming out to the float, reading in Adirondack chairs. Each of us would have our hour with Klein, each would be asked similar questions and expected to talk until we felt better, or until Klein felt better about us, and recommended, in his professional opinion, that we return home— back to our husbands or our wives, back to our lovers, our mothers or fathers. We were not many, but we were a collection of misery.

"The delivery room," he said.

"Yes, I guess that's what they still call it. The delivery room or the operating room or wherever it was that they had rolled me into. I don't know," I said. "I was drugged. You know. They give you what you need for the pain."

"So you don't remember?"

"I remember," I said.

"What, then?"

"The quiet," I said, a bit agitated. Hadn't we begun here?

"Explain it," he said.

Always, with Klein, it came to this: the feeling that he walked me in circles, like a trainer of something wild, a horse that needs calming, around and around, until the horse stops bucking from sheer exhaustion or boredom or both. It was not the first time we had come to this, this question. Believe me, I had explained it more than once.

I sighed. Sometimes one really does in these situations.

"Well," I began, "when Rebecca was born, it was all sound and light. I remember the round white light over me, the sound of her screaming cry, and how the doctors were talking about something else when she was born and how they continued talking after letting me know that she was here, a girl, beautiful, all the things they say. There was chatter. A continuous chatter. I lay there in the middle of a place where people were working."

I found myself drifting. I always did around this part. I wanted to turn around, to see what Klein would see if he looked past me out the window. I wanted to smoke, but Klein would not allow this. And so I continued.

"But with this baby there was no sound. Nothing. Just this large silence. I knew immediately that something was terribly wrong, but no one told me. They just took her away, quickly, telling me she was a girl, and that I should rest. But they had stopped talking among themselves, and they worked with this kind of steadiness and serious-ness that felt wrong. I wanted to scream, 'What is it?' But I felt too tired, and so I shut my eyes and slept."

"Yes?" he said.

"I wish I had said something," I said.

He paused here, as he always would. I know he believed I told the story for my benefit more than his, that somehow in the telling of it I was curing myself, but I am not sure. I think I told him because I wanted it known. I wanted another person to take it with them, to keep it, that sense of the quiet of a delivery room, those bright lights. Does this make sense to you? I wanted someone else to carry my story with them. I wanted it gone from me.

"What?" he said at last. "What would you have said?"

I hated this part of it. "I would have asked for a cigarette," I said. Klein smiled his reptilian smile.

"Then what?" he said.

"God knows," I said. "Perhaps I would have asked what was

wrong, and then knowing would have asked where they kept the sleeping pills. How does that sound?"

"About right," said Klein. "You eventually found both."

"Right," I said. "No heart, just shards of one. Not the kind we draw on valentines, certainly. Not the handful of black blood they would have shaken at the gods, the heart of a warrior, or a hunter, or a learned man, but something flimsy, I imagine. Yellow. A nightgown of a heart."

Klein waited a moment. I had never spoken in such a way, so out of character. He attempted, rather badly, to hide his interest. "And the other?"

"The other?" I said.

"The pills," he said.

"Oh, that other," I said. "Well, of course. Those are always easy to find."

"Took some looking, though."

"Well," I said.

Klein tapped his pencil against his desk. I wondered if the constant shaking of his leg might be a form of self-medication — he had no Klein to walk him around and around in circles and so he shook it out.

"The baby did have a heart. It just wasn't a strong one," he said, leaning forward.

"It's a better metaphor my way," I said.

"*Touché*," he said.

"And let's admit, I only made a halfhearted, pun intended, attempt at the latter."

"You didn't want to abandon Rebecca."

"What am I doing here?"

A Place on a Lake 1966

"You felt you needed to be here for Rebecca."

"I need to be here for both of them."

"Who's them?"

"Rebecca, the baby."

"The baby is dead."

"The baby."

"The baby, Marion, is dead."

You see, he believed he had to convince me of this; that I was not, as they said at the time, "accepting the reality of the situation." But of course I knew.

I shared my cabin with a woman named Mrs. Whitehead. She always identified herself as such, and I always called her that. She must have been sixty at the time, but I thought of her as ancient. She had silver white hair and tremendously sad eyes and a short strand of pearls she asked me to clasp every morning. She smelled of that powder no one uses anymore. I liked her immediately. I think of her because, leaving the cabin, I would first hear the screen door slam and then Mrs.Whitehead calling out for me to be careful of the sun. She said it every morning, and every day she spent the day indoors, sitting in a rocking chair beyond the cast of the sun through our screen door, waiting her turn with Klein, the meals in the main cabin.

Once at the lakeshore, I would roll out my blanket and sit close enough to the water to put my toes in. Someone had told me there were perch in the lake, and that they would bite. I'm not sure of this. They had me on a type of medication that kept me drowsy. I would lie in the sun, sleeping on and off, thinking of you and of the baby and of, from time to time, your father. I knew the baby was dead. I knew what I had done was selfish, though I did not regret it. If I had succeeded I might have paved the way for you both to be happier. As it was, it was almost as if I could see the future spread out before me. I knew the unhappiness of my life, could taste it.

"My baby is dead," I said to Klein.

This is what he was after, and I knew the sooner I got to it, the sooner I would be released, permitted to return to the edge of the lake, where I would spend the rest of the day until they rang the bell for dinner and the fireflies began to appear, like a hundredfold spectacle, in the pines across the lake.

"Come on," Mrs. Whitehead would say, coming up behind me, tapping my shoulder. "The sun's going down."

"Thank you," I said.

"Dinner," she would say, nodding toward the main cabin and the others walking toward it across the lawn. Then I would stand and she would turn, holding the two ends of the short strand of pearls as close together as she could reach with them. I had found out, when I first arrived, that her youngest boy had been wounded early in Vietnam, friendly fire, and he could no longer walk or feed himself and that she cared for him. Well, she would stand there very still, not saying a word, just waiting, and I would click the clasp into place, all the while smelling the powdery smell of her and the sudden cold from the lake.

The dining hall tables had place cards. They liked to keep us circulating, so no one would feel left out, excluded. Had they known us well, they would have known that that is how we arrived and how we would leave. If I had to lump us together, I would say we were one great breathing loneliness. That is how it felt in that room for dinner, a vast cavernous room with mooseheads or deerheads or some sort of dead things mounted on wood boards, circling high above us. If we looked up we could see their dead eyes glistening with candlelight.

A Place on a Lake 1966

We would hear from Klein every evening after dessert. A quick lecture, pep talk. He would stand before us, in front of one of the most gigantic fireplaces I had ever seen. It ran the whole length of the room and had been built from hundreds of round stones. There, in front of the black mouth of it, he shouted to get our attention, though there was no need; we were not making what they call a din. In fact, we rarely spoke to one another. But there Klein appeared every night, bright as a penny, his spectacles polished.

"Ladies and gentlemen," he always began. "Good evening."

"Good evening," we replied.

"On the whole we are doing better," he said. "I am pleased, quite pleased. I see among us acts of daring and bravery that would have been unimaginable weeks ago. We have set a course and we are on it. Every day each one of us excels in what is joyous. Life. Indeed!" he said. "We are on our way."

He began the applause, and we followed him. Then he continued with announcements of various scheduled activities. Often, when I watched him, turned in my chair with the rest of the guests, responding, applauding, I would not listen to him speaking at all. It was like a strange trick I could suddenly do; I had found the ability to block my ears, to close myself off so entirely that the room might have erupted with laughter, for all I knew. I separated myself from the noise as cleanly as a baby is separated from its mother's umbilical cord. I had cut myself free. I would find myself in a crowded room, warm with breath and speech, and hear absolutely nothing. Those times I often wondered about that fireplace, wondered at the person who had come up with such an idea. To imagine a room lit length to length with fire. The wonder of that.

Well we were, somewhat. On the road, I mean. On our way, or however Klein would put it. After all, when your father picked me up three weeks later, he said I had not looked that radiant in years, said he understood that it had been difficult, but that he believed I had come out of it with flying colors.

Flying colors.

I gave him no reason to think differently. You see, I had begun to apply that trick, the trick of blocking my ears, stepping out of wherever I was back into that absolute, stark white silence, over the course of any day, so that I could, if I chose, sit at dinner with you and your father and hear nothing of what you might say to me. It was as if I had learned how to be two Marions: one acting in her present life, one arrested in a past moment. I know that you have suffered from this, Rebecca, and I am terribly, terribly sorry. But I want you to understand. Somehow I had no alternative.

The night before I left, I woke to find Mrs. Whitehead standing over me. At first, in the dark, I had no idea who she was and thought that she might be the ghost of your grandmother come to give me directions on how to continue with my life. That passed quickly, though, and I saw that, indeed, it was Mrs. Whitehead who stood directly above me, looking down, her large glassy eyes fine white pools in the dark.

"Mrs. Whitehead?" I whispered. I sat up. "Sit down," I said.

I moved my legs over to give her some room. We slept in narrow camp cots, not unlike the kind they use in the army.

"I'm sorry," she said. "I can't sleep."

"Quite all right," I said, and I meant it. I believe I had only drowsed off a few moments before. I should not have to tell you that sleeping did not come easily to me, and each night felt like a long distance crossed.

"I'm sorry," she said again. Then, "Mrs. Clark, I'm going for a swim."

"Mrs. Whitehead?"

"Out there. You know, in the lake. Have you tried the lake?"

"No," I said. "I believe it's cold."

"It's very cold," she said.

"You've been?" I said.

"No," she said. "Well, before."

I noticed that she had removed her short strand of pearls, and that her bare neck, exposed above the collar of her nightgown, looked quite old. I don't think Mrs. Whitehead had ever said so many consecutive words to me.

"Will you come?" she said.

"Of course," I said.

I followed Mrs. Whitehead out the screen door, making sure that it did not slam behind us as we stepped into that exquisite night landscape that is yours when all others sleep. The sky had a purplish cast to it. Loons glided across the water, then dropped beneath and disappeared. The pines appeared to be a black mountain. At the shore, Mrs. Whitehead lifted her nightgown over her head, and I saw her transform in the dark to a large white animal. She stepped in and sunk down— the water, I imagined, closing up over her. But, again, that silence. I walked fast to where she had been and took off my own nightgown. As you know, your mother is quite modest, and to be standing on the lakeshore stark naked in the middle of a hot night in Virginia, any one of the other guests able to see me simply by looking out their dusty screens, would normally have set me running to hide behind the nearest pine. Not that night. I felt somehow renewed by the simple gesture of Mrs. Whitehead's offer; it was as if she knew that we were in this together and, being accomplices, we should act as such and break the rules. That night I felt sure of myself, and if Klein had appeared, standing on the big porch off the main cabin smoking his pipe as he sometimes would after dinner, I might have grabbed his hand and invited him to join us.

The water was cold, frigid at first, before I unclenched my arms and fists and began to really swim. To swim! Awkwardly, then not. I went deep. Touched the muddy bottom. I scissored my legs and rolled on my back in a backstroke. Then I sank, again. Opening my eyes, I saw nothing through the haze of that depth. Nothing. I sank farther, pushed myself down—lay flat on the bottom, kicking my legs as if fighting off a slew of angry perch. I held my breath and shut my eyes and stayed as long as I could stand it. And when I came up, bursting with a sudden whoosh into the night—my ears filled sound, with sound!, my lungs tight as my heart—dear Mrs. Whitehead was already there, kneeling on the float with both arms out to pull me up. I am not sure how long we lay on the float, the two of us side by side. Women were just beginning to speak of their lives. We had all abided by some silent code. We spoke of our children and our husbands and our husbands' jobs. We played Bridge. We got drunk on Friday and Saturday nights at dinner parties. I am sure it had been the same for Mrs. Whitehead. Neither of us said a word for a very long time.

"I tried it, too," Mrs. Whitehead finally said.

I may have fallen asleep, I'm not sure. I know I startled.

"I'm sorry?" I said. I rolled halfway over to look at her. I must admit, I wished I had carried a towel above my head through the water. My understanding of my own nakedness with a stranger, albeit a stranger I had shared a cabin with for weeks, had begun to take form. I brought my legs up, crossed my arms over my knees. Mrs. Whitehead seemed entirely oblivious. She lifted her head, looked at me. Then she made a gesture I have not cared to remember before, sweeping one hand across her wrist as if to slice it open.

"That," she said, returning her attention to the sky.

"Oh," I said.

"I failed," she said.

"Yes?" I said.

"So I tried this," she said, bringing one hand up and across her neck in the way the movie people do, to mean cut.

She sat up then and let her head fall back. Mrs. Whitehead, naked in the moonlight, had stepped out of the age of beauty. It was difficult to sit so close, so directly close. "This," she said, aware of my inattention. She pointed to her throat. I leaned in and saw: tiny stitches.

"You cut your own throat?" I said.

"In a manner of speaking," she said. Now she mimicked my position: knees up, arms crossed. "It's a long story. One I have told to our good Doctor Klein so often I would rather not repeat it here."

"Fine," I said.

The light had begun to catch across the lake, so the pines now were defined and the boulders of the point and even the lakeshore, where we could see our nightgowns, folded, like patient skins we would soon need to step back into.

"I go home today," I offered.

"Understood," Mrs. Whitehead said. "Doctor Klein told me."

"Klein knows all, sees all. He's like the Wizard," I said.

"And this is Oz?" Mrs. Whitehead said, and laughed. Perhaps it was the sound of it, a real chortle, that attracted him, but at the moment of her laugh a loon appeared, popping up from the lake so close we could see the outline of his feathers. Loons, as you may know, are notoriously lonesome birds. You will never catch them coming close for bread crumbs, and always, just when you believe you might be able to approach one in a canoe, he will disappear, dropping fast into the water, rising in a place far beyond your imagination.

Mrs. Whitehead caught her breath, and then the two of us sat dead still, watching as the loon paddled even closer and then circled around the float. We turned to follow him and saw that we had been facing west, and that behind us the sun rose through clouds that fanned its color. Against this, the loon held, a silhouette, then cried and disappeared back into the lake water. Mrs. Whitehead and I remained watching, as one always does, refusing to believe that a bird as wondrous as that could so easily move out of our sight. And though we waited, the loon never reappeared. I thought of it swimming, how it pushed itself through the dark of the deeper lake water, its feet tangled with the muck and the rotting root of the lake bed.

Your father picked me up that morning. He arrived in the station wagon by way of the long dirt road through the pines and parked behind the main cabin. Klein had his office there, and your father, before finding me, was required to meet with him and to hear his analysis. He has never told me precisely what Klein said, but in the years since then he has, on certain angry occasions, said Klein said as much and so forth. I've paid little attention to that. I can imagine what Klein took from our sessions. I know I took the light reflected in his spectacles and his nervous knee.

Anyway, Mrs. Whitehead and I had returned to our cabin only a few hours before. We swam back quickly, slipping our nightgowns over our heads once on shore and running to the cabin like boarding school girls. I can hear that laugh of hers, how it echoed out through the early morning, waking, I am sure, a number of the other guests. We let the screen door slam and got back into our beds. There was a warmth to my bed that felt nothing short of delicious, and I pulled the wool blanket up over my nose, my hair still wet, and slept the sleep of a survivor.

Your father's knocking woke me up. "Marion?" I heard. "Sweetheart?"

"Shhh," I said. "Mrs. Whitehead."

He tiptoed in.

"Where are you?" he said.

"Here," I said.

I must admit, I felt glad to see him, awkward, as he was, in the middle of a dark cabin, his short sleeve button-down decidedly new.

"Darling, here," I said.

He turned and found me. I did not want to get out of bed. I felt somehow safest where I lay. If he could have lifted me and carried me out, put me into the back of the station wagon, my nightgown warm, the wet-wood smell of the float still strong on me, I would have been fine.

We kissed, and he tried to hug me beneath the covers. Then he said he had a surprise. That you were there, too. I'm sure you have little memory of it, but there you were, waiting for your cue to come in, to jump on my cot and shout hello, which you did again and again, waking Mrs. Whitehead. Your father and I took you to the lakeshore, where you sailed a boat he jury-rigged from birch bark and pinecones. You swam, your father holding you around the waist as you kicked, then with one hand on your back as you attempted to float. By midmorning, we were all tired. Your father suggested we get on the road. We would be home before dark.

Goodbye, I said, to Klein and the others. Goodbye, I said to Mrs. Whitehead. She squeezed my shoulder. Goodbye, she said.

I am not sure how much longer Mrs. Whitehead intended to stay. In truth, I knew little about her. I had heard of her son's condition, and that she had come from Cleveland. She told me she had two other boys, grown and married, living not so far from her. Her husband had retired and now spent most of his time building model airplanes in the basement.

I was halfway to the screen door, your father behind, carrying my bags, you already out constructing some parallel camp of pine needles and bark and pebbles, when I heard Mrs. Whitehead clear her throat.

"Mrs. Clark?" she said. I stopped and your father stopped and she stepped toward us into the sun that came through the screen door. Have I told you she was a handsome woman? Though her eyes were an odd shape, her hair had turned the color of gray that is a color. She wore terrible clothes, things you might see on an English woman in her garden. Every blouse had a ruffled neck, every skirt reached the wrong length—yet they were crisply ironed and to them she always added her pearls.

Which, I saw immediately, was the reason she had stopped me. Her hands were up on either side of her neck, behind her neck, as she approached me, as if she were attempting to tie a bib. I don't believe she said anything other than my name before she turned, hunching her shoulders a bit so that I could more easily reach the clasp.

There are times when a gesture can break your heart. I clicked the clasp into place, then smoothed the fabric of her blouse with my hand. I would have liked to touch her scars, but we were only brief acquaintances.

Baltimore

1975

H ere they are: three on the beach staring out toward Robert's camera, a stranger focusing the lens. "Stand upwind," Robert tells the stranger. "Your back to the sun." He puts his arm around Marion and his hand on Rebecca's shoulder. The stranger steps up a bit, steadies Robert's camera, and, as she does, the sun sparks a sliver of light across the Gulf, a streak so bright that Robert draws Marion close to him, squeezes the hard flesh that wraps Rebecca's shoulder bone.

"I'm bored," Rebecca says. She is seventeen and frequently is.

"Smile," says Robert.

"Cheese," says the stranger. Marion smiles, focusing on the black line of the jetty sinking into the Gulf. There, dark seaweed-laced waves break, and abandoned nets, long snagged on the rooty bottom, repeatedly fill and empty.

▼

A week or so later, Rebecca hundreds of miles away—returned to the school from which she will soon graduate, striding across the makeshift stage—Marion drives to the drugstore to purchase a box of Nicorettes. She has tried to quit smoking before, and each morning that she awakens with the dry feeling of smoke etched in her throat she promises she will stop again. Not so long ago she went to a hypnotist, a balding man who gestured toward a cracked red leather chair and told her to empty her heart. She sat for a few minutes and watched the spot on the wall he told her to watch and listened to the words he said, or sang, because in no time the words had lost their meaning and were no longer words but sounds. Then she spoke. She told him of the baby, of Klein and Mrs. Whitehead. Of Dorothy. She told him how she had moved fifteen times in twenty years of marriage. She told him of the man who came to the door of their farmhouse when she was a little girl. This was the early forties. Depression, she said.

The man, she told the hypnotist, said, I have nothing but the clothes on my back, but I will play the piano for food. Mother let him in. She would do that sometimes. Surprise you with kindness to strangers. The man walked in like a scared animal. We did have a piano for him to play. Cynthia took lessons. The man sat down, and Mother went back to the kitchen, where meat cooked in the oven and vegetables boiled. You have to understand we were poor. Democrats among Republicans. Mother said it took no money to be clean, to have manners; still, when Robert and I went to General Westcott's for dinner, I had no idea what fork went with what dish.

Anyway, the man opened the piano case and flexed his fingers. I watched from the corner of the room. I had gotten used to the bums who would come and beg, making Mother shake her head no and shut the door. But this man sat at our piano and played, scales from the low octaves up and then a sonata Cynthia later said was Chopin. She appeared from nowhere. Then Mother came back in. The three of us stood transfixed, listening. We did not feel sorry for the man who owned nothing but the clothes on his back. Because he could play unlike anyone we had ever heard play before, we felt sorry for ourselves, for having only meat and vegetables to offer—

Here the hypnotist had interrupted Marion. No, he had said. I mean empty your heart of the reasons why you smoke.

Oh, Marion said, and shrugged. Habit?

Now Marion, who once in the drugstore has remembered that she has not yet picked up the photographs from the family vacation, watches as the girl behind the counter shuffles through a shoe box of developed film and hands her a heavy packet. Marion cannot wait to look through the pictures and stands, chewing a Nicorette, beyond the swinging doors of the drugstore. Here are Robert and Rebecca in familiar places—sitting at the three-legged table in the living room of their rented cottage, in front of the ice cream shop, on the beach. Then Marion turns to a photograph of a stranger, her face unnaturally white, eyes red, her image distorted by what appears to be an explosion of light behind her, pulling her backward, sucking her in.

Who is she? Marion thinks, momentarily imagining the stranger a ghost of a dead relative, or some kind of angel sent to warn her.

"Who shot this?" Robert says that evening.

"You did," Marion says, chewing a Nicorette. The taste is fine at first, before it deadens.

"The sun must have shifted," he says, passing the photograph back to her.

Marion looks at him, chewing.

"We promised we'd send it. It was an exchange. Her picture for ours, remember? You took her address, didn't you?"

"God knows," Robert says. "I can't even find my golf clubs."

The photograph of the stranger makes its way around the house, perched, for an afternoon, atop the credit card receipts and loose change on Marion and Robert's bedroom bureau, then surfacing in the hollowed-out back of a ceramic frog Marion cast and fired while enrolled in The Art of Handcrafts at the Baltimore Community College.

Marion had also enrolled in The Art of Japanese Flower Arrangement, The Art of Mexican Cooking, and The Art of Simple Refurbishing. It had been Rebecca's idea. Something to get her going, Rebecca had said. To take her mind off things.

"My mind has long been off things," Marion said.

They sat on the flagstone patio eating sharp cheddar on melba toast and drinking white wine, their feet on the wrought-iron picnic table. Marion's nails, Rebecca remarked, were the color of the melba toast.

"Nonsense," Marion said. "This is Burnt Copper. No. Coppery Peach. That's it. Coppery Peach."

"Oh," Rebecca said, and took a sip of wine.

Marion lit a cigarette in the way that she would after a few glasses of wine. It was early November, and the trees, quite suddenly bare, left a melancholy view before her of what seemed like endless houses with endless garages and endless kitchen windows. They had been here about a year, and she had come to know some of her neighbors—though with Rebecca away at school there seemed little reason to make a great effort.

"Dorothy called this the blue hour," Marion said, remembering.

"Dorothy?" Rebecca said.

"Someone," Marion said. "You played with her boys."

Rebecca looked at Marion and shook her head. "Where?"

"Rochester," Marion said.

"Rochester? God, Rochester." Rebecca put down her glass. She had had too much to drink, she knew, and now wondered how she would make it through dinner and the slow hours before bedtime. "I love you, Mother," she said, unexpectedly. "But you've got to do something. Quit smoking, for one. And cut your hair. You're looking poodleish again."

M arion went to the hairdresser's the next day. There she saw the community college catalog and decided to take action. Once enrolled, she had gone faithfully to each class, creating, in addition to the porcelain frog, a beaded leather vest and a découpage handbag. It was while enrolled in The Art of Simple Refurbishing that she had seen the advertisement for the hypnotist posted on the campus bulletin board. One thing will lead to another, she would have said, if Rebecca had asked her. But Rebecca had forgotten her suggestions as soon as she made them.

▼

Several months after the family vacation, Robert, settled in the living room on the couch with the trumpet vine pattern, reading the newspaper, looks down to see the stranger on a stack of books beneath the glass coffee table. "My God," he says to Marion, who has been sitting beside him, thinking. "Can't we get rid of her?"

How did she find her way here? Marion thinks, then is distracted by the Wyeth picture book on which the stranger rests. She thought she had misplaced that years ago: the year Rebecca turned three, or the year they moved to the house where the muskrats killed the ducks, the year they built the ranch, or the blue clapboard; the year they planted the willow.

"It must have been the new cleaning woman," Marion says. She chews on her Nicorette, glad for its rubbery feel. It has been nearly six weeks since she smoked a cigarette, though she believes she has not smoked her last one. She will smoke again, she knows. The question is when. In a sense, the suspense lessens the edge. It is as if she has a secret that she will soon tell.

"I'll get rid of her," Marion says, then goes back to thinking.

Marion awakens in the middle of the night. She is tired, but restless. Random thoughts and ideas bump and whirl in the dark of her side of the bed. In some place far from where she is, she hears the man playing the piano, Chopin, and sees her younger self standing with her sister and her mother, listening. They are like a family portrait, three women who came from what they were doing to listen.

Downstairs, in the Spanish chest in the dining room, is a pack of cigarettes kept for emergencies. She hears Robert breathing loud and deep, aware that if she turned on the light she would see his hands folded on his chest.

She gets up and follows the hallway to the top of the stairs. From here, she can see the edge of the pale yellow dining room, the edge of the cherry dining room table set in the middle. Behind it, the Spanish chest.

The clock ticks on the mantle. Marion listens to it as she walks down the stairs, passing the framed photographs that line the wall: photographs taken in all their other places: Huntington, St. Louis, Wilmington, Charlottesville, Houston, Tokyo, Cleveland, Atlanta, Kansas City, Detroit, Rochester, Norfolk, Durham, Philadelphia, Baltimore, each one Robert promising would be the last.

Marion opens the top drawer of the Spanish chest, careful not to make a sound. She understands that this is absurd, that nothing would wake Robert, that Rebecca is not here to see, that she is, virtually, alone. But still, she sneaks as if escaping: opening the French doors, stepping onto the flagstone patio. It is early March, and, though the days are warmer, the nights are still bitter and damp. She wraps her robe more tightly around her, reaches into her pocket for matches. She feels the hard edge of paper and pulls out the photograph of the stranger. "Hello," she says, as if greeting a friend. "How did you find your way here?" The stranger looks out at her through the dark, her face a flash of white. She says nothing. "Poor baby," Marion says, knowing that the stranger is not at her best, that she has been in unfamiliar territory for weeks, that she will remain here, shuttled from place to place, until no one bothers to move her anymore and she is forgotten at the bottom of a drawer.

Marion tucks her back into her pocket, finds her matches, and lights a cigarette, the fire audible, oxygen feeding the flame that burns the tobacco. She sucks in the smoke and shuts her eyes. She thinks of the man's sonata, how he looked in his old coat. No shoes, or a poor excuse for shoes, dirty fingernails, his face peppered with stubble, but playing to beat the band, knowing, if just for that moment, that he was heard.

"Cheese," Marion says, letting the smoke out.

REBECCA

Jamaica

1978

Down near the cliffs is the bigger hut, where guests sit on chairs or lie in hammocks strung from bamboo poles. The hammocks look like the fish nets in the market, fish nets filled with wet silver fish. In the midafternoon, when it is too hot to swim or to sit on the cliff or to walk in the hills where white crosses, bone dry, mark graves, Rebecca lies next to her boyfriend, Jack. The sun has given her a stronger resemblance to Marion—her hair bleached to a lighter shade of brown. But she is older than Marion was at twenty, suspicious in a way that is clear in repose. She reads Simone de Beauvoir and believes this means something. What, she isn't sure.

She has convinced Jack to come to this island; he is not a traveler. He is simply a boy Rebecca may be in love with. It could go either way, and it does, depending, shifting as easily as the hot afternoon breezes that strand tourists in doldrums. Rebecca had loved Jack when she first let him into her dorm room, when they both felt much younger, but she had not participated in the making of love that night. Instead, she lay there wondering, staring past him to the ceiling. It was the sounds of him she would remember, and his smell, still on her long after he had walked back to his own room, buttoning his coat against the winter wind. Rebecca thought of that night as a promissory note that had come due; she knew she must pay, sooner or later. To be beautiful, Marion had once told her, cinching some tight patent leathers, requires pain.

Rebecca takes off her robe and feels the breeze from the water blowing over her. She closes her eyes, thinking of how, earlier, the owner of the place, the one married to the movie star, has told her she should be in the movies.

"What are you thinking?" Jack asks.

It is quiet in the heat. The other guests might be sleeping. They hang like white stones in webbed nets.

"Nothing," Rebecca says. Then, "Marion. I was thinking of Marion—how, if I were in the movies, Marion would think it was great. She'd think I was swell."

"You are swell," Jack says.

At night, a scorpion crawls on the zebra-skin spread. Rebecca watches its tail whip back and forth, angry. The heat has her sweating down the insides of her thighs; she has felt this riding bareback, when horsehair and white sweat clung to her skin. Jack looks at her hard. "He's right," he says. "You could be in the movies."

▼

When it rains, the owner stays under the awning of his porch raised high off the ground on thick bamboo stilts. His wife, the movie star, sits in front of a mirror propped against the porch railing, drawing on, then wiping off, tiny black moles. She dips her fingers into bowls at her feet, then spreads a thick paste on the points of her elbows. A chameleon races up the movie star's leg; she lets the chameleon stay.

In the bigger hut, the guests play backgammon and chess, the empty hammocks lightly slapped by the wind. Jack sleeps on the zebra-skin spread.

The owner watches Rebecca swim. She swims alone, though she imagines Jack swimming next to her, his pale legs pushing him through the weight of the water, his pale hands pointed in blades.

The owner sits near the white robe she has left on the cliff by the six carved steps that lead into the ocean. He waves. She stops and treads water.

Later he will touch her cold skin.

"Don't shudder," he will say. "Learn control."

He will reach behind him to his dirty cloths; it is very late, the middle of the night.

"Don't move," he will say, bringing up the paring knife. "Don't shudder," he repeats.

Rebecca will lie back on the cliffs as he presses the knife point into her skin, marking her with benign circles.

"My mother," she will tell him. "Wants me to do everything she never did. You can imagine the possibilities," she says.

The owner will laugh and nod. "I can imagine," he says then. But for now, he simply waves.

In the morning, two new guests arrive. They wear long cotton pants and sit in the shade of the thatched roof of the bigger hut, early in the day through sunset. The man lifts the woman's shirt and spreads white lotion across her back. Her back looks like a child's back.

The new man has the gray eyes of the blind, or the eyes of the fish who stay beneath the cliff wall. Because no one can see them, they have faded to nothing. This Rebecca has heard from the owner. Because no one can see the fish, they have faded to skeleton bones and those eyes, the owner tells her. It is the reason you must be in the movies, he says. You must be in the movies to be seen.

At night, Jack checks the zebra skin for scorpions. He is naked, and the soft hairs on his back and neck have turned blond. Earlier, Rebecca rubbed lemon on the roots of his hair, squeezing the rind to get most of the juice. But his hair stayed the same color, drying with the hard seeds of lemon.

Jack sleeps. Rebecca rolls over on the zebra skin and places her bare feet on the floor. She puts on the white robe laid across the bamboo stool and ties the robe tight with its sash. She is not far from the cliff and the six carved steps to the ocean, not far from the owner, who sits on his porch, his cigarette orange in the dark.

They move together to the cliff wall and Rebecca unties the sash and the robe slips off her shoulders. She feels as if she is already in the movies, acting a role she has learned in the dark. They lie down together, and he counts again what will have to be fixed, outlining the hard raised skin of a scar on her hip.

In his other hand, the owner's cigarette burns to ash.

"This will be difficult," he says, tracing a birthmark on her arm.

Rebecca tells him of a teacher whom Marion had had fired, a man who would ask students to recite the names of the planets—first out from the sun and then back—while holding a lit match between their fingers. "Mercury Venus Earth Mars Jupiter Saturn Uranus Neptune Pluto Pluto Neptune Uranus Saturn Jupiter Mars Earth Venus Mercury," she says now, the fire closing in on her fingertips.

In the morning, Rebecca walks down the dry dirt road to the market in town.

"How much do you love me?" Jack asks as she's leaving, and she holds out her hands as if measuring a wide distance, a fish story.

A pack of young boys walks behind her. They have things to sell, but she is heading to the market to buy what the movie star buys, to buy the paste she keeps at her feet, so she ignores them. When she reaches the outskirts of the market, she hears the sound of barter. Sacks of powders and grains lean against the tent poles. Silver fish flap on newspapers spread over the ground. A cluster of old women in black dresses stand near the place where she goes, where she has followed the wife of the owner, the movie star, before. She has watched them touch the movie star's face, rub her hands, give her the things that they keep in their pockets. She has watched them huddle beneath the tree like black crows. It is a kind of tree that grows here, a small tree with low brown branches, awkward, hunched, as if wanting to go back to the ground. The old women have hung the tree with mirrors, hundreds of mirrors no bigger than quarters. It is what she walks to.

As she approaches, the women move away, encircling the tree in black. In the reflection of the mirrors, there are thousands of them, black specks of pepper.

"Yes?" one says.

Rebecca wants to see herself in the tree; she wants to see what the owner sees when he says this will take some time, when he says there is work to be done.

She takes off her bracelets one by one. Then she unbuttons her dress until it hangs wide open. She pushes the sleeves of her dress off her arms and shakes her dress to her ankles.

Someone runs for someone. Jack arrives, short of breath. He seems unsure of what to do, whom to call. This is not like her, he says to the cluster of old women in black dresses. This is really not like her. He walks Rebecca back to the bigger hut, settling her into one of the hammocks.

"Keep her out of it," they have told him. "Keep her in the shade."

The new guests are there too, the woman asleep in a hammock near Rebecca, the man sitting in a chair. The woman's head rests on a hat, flattened against the web of the hammock's netting. The things I could tell her, Rebecca thinks. How these hats, on sale on the beaches, are woven from the strong grass that grows from the graves in the hills, and that it is not strong grass at all but the hairs of the dead, dry hairs pushed through the dirt in the hills of white crosses.

In the evening it is cooler. The new man and woman are somewhere else. Rebecca is alone with Jack. She lies in a hammock while Jack pretends to read, his head bent slightly over his book, over one page, his thumb and middle finger lifting the page as if to turn to the next. He sits near the lantern, its blue flame low. Occasionally, he looks up and stares at the ocean, his eyes narrowed as if to focus on something that was once there, something he has glimpsed and lost.

"From now on," he says to Rebecca, "stay close. Will you promise?"

"Of course," she says, though later she lifts her bare feet from the zebra-skin spread and stands up from the bed. Outside, the wind blows hard. She walks to the top of the six carved steps and sits. The waves are strong and break fast, drawing into the water all that is loose or weak. She watches as a rat slips down the cliff wall and disappears into the dark, its tail the last part of it to vanish. She will soon feel the owner. It will happen this way: he will come up behind her and dive into the dark where the rat disappeared. She will stay where she is until he tugs her ankles. The second pull will be that, a pull, and then suddenly she will be in, her back scraping the cliff wall, her breath caught in her throat.

Florence

1980

The boys toss stones into a circle drawn in the dirt and hop in and out of the circle. When Romeo walks by tapping his stick, the boys throw stones at Romeo's feet.

Romeo follows sound.

If the sound is a bird, Romeo flies; if the sound is a snake Romeo crawls; if the sound is a cricket, Romeo jumps.

Romeo's eyes are white and roll in their sockets.

Romeo taps through the aisles of Mr. Dolce's store. In the store are rows of red and yellow fruit and rows of white BiC shavers and rows of candy in plastic wrappers. Taped to the front glass window, Jesus hangs over the tomatoes.

Mr. Dolce gives Romeo orange juice in a can.

The boys have borrowed a car and driven to the Piazza Michelangelo to walk on the stone wall like tightrope walkers, balancing their steps with their arms held out from their sides. They see Romeo tapping his way from the city and drive in the car to Romeo and say, Romeo, get into the car. We will drive you some places and show you some things.

The boys take Romeo to the front steps of the Duomo, where the American lady Lise sells postcards five for one dollar or ten thousand lira.

"Lise, look what we have," the boys say.

Lise tapes a postcard of Michelangelo to Romeo's back and spins Romeo around and around.

The pigeons line the corn seller Mario's arms as Mario shouts, "For ten cents, I will sell you my picture to tape to the backs of those boys."

But the boys have gone, their car careening up the steep curves that lead to the Piazza Michelangelo. Below them, the Arno twists through the shadows cast by the red-clay roofs and church domes of the city. The brown river moves slowly, heavy with silt and the dyes from the sweater factory up north. Shirts hang in rows of three above the water, pinned to the clotheslines that crisscross the Ponte Vecchio.

At the Caffè Boboli, a reporter from Chicago orders his first drink.

"What is there to do here?" he asks the waiter.

The waiter removes the white cloth draped over his left forearm and wipes his hands, then he shrugs and walks back to the kitchen doorway to stand where the other waiters stand.

Down from the Duomo belltower a monk descends. In his pocket is a postcard of Michelangelo he will send to his mother in Naples. He has found the postcard on the wide stone steps of the Duomo—Michelangelo flat on his back, eyes skyward. How the monk misses his mother, who sits by her window counting pigeons as if they were messages from God.

Mr. Dolce pulls the grate down over the front glass window then locks his store for the night. At home, Mrs. Dolce slices garlic with a knife.

Florence 1980

Romeo props his stick between his legs, leaning his head back, his white eyes rolling left then right like white marbles on a track. The boys stop the car and say, Me, oh my, look what we have here.

Rebecca shaves her legs sitting on the stone lip of the fountain in the center of the Piazza Michelangelo. An Iranian market seller kneels before her.

"Miss America," he says. "Whatever you ask."

The boys shove Romeo out of the car and drive away quickly, careening down the steep curves that lead up to the Piazza Michelangelo.

The reporter from Chicago totals his check, then pulls out a wad of lira he has pushed into the pocket of his trousers.

When you're a Jet you're a Jet all the way from your first cigarette to your last dying day, sing the tourists.

Mr. Dolce opens the door to his apartment and sneaks toward his wife who stands with her back to the door. He kisses her neck like a bandit, sliding his hand underneath her apron and between her legs.

Michelangelo and da Vinci walk over the Ponte Vecchio, discussing their work. They pause and look at the reflection of the city that quivers on the surface of the water like the silhouette of a sculpture. With a swift jerk Michelangelo tosses his brush into the Arno, the water turning blue then rose red then gold. Da Vinci says the color of the water comes from the old pigment embedded deep in the crown of the bristles of Michelangelo's brush, but Michelangelo says no. Michelangelo says this is a message from God.

▼

Romeo reaches the edge of the Piazza Michelangelo and taps his way over the stone wall. On the other side of the stone wall, the hill overgrown with fern slopes downward.

The boys drive to a party in the city where there will be music and dancing and food. They arrive late, and the hostess says please do not come in.

Sometimes, because da Vinci does not have a mother, Michelangelo has trouble consoling his friend. Michelangelo dreams of angels in all corners of his house while his mother cooks his meals and washes his smocks. Da Vinci ruins his eyes sketching in the dark.

On the sloping hill in the fern Romeo stabs his stick, then stumbles. The orange juice from Mr. Dolce has made him thirsty; he follows the sound and the stench of the Arno.

Lise closes her postcard stand and counts her dollars and lira. She thinks of returning to the stone mansion where the fascists have burned out the inside and written their names in red paint across the floor. There, in the early morning, the cypress that line the road whisper stories of the fascists, and the wind blows as the shepherd leads the sheep away.

Bells ring in the valley.

The Iranian market seller asks Rebecca if she is a virgin.

She laughs.

He sighs.

"I will do anything you want," he says. "In Iran, before the revolution, I was a doctor. A surgeon specializing in cancer," he tells her.

Rebecca tilts her head and listens. She has met the Iranian market seller in the street behind the mausoleum where the finger bones of the Medicis crumble against velvet. From the Iranian market seller she bought a leather jacket for herself and leather gloves for Marion.

▼

Florence 1980

The reporter from Chicago drinks a warm glass of Scotch in his room. From his window he sees the arched dome of the Duomo lit from behind with blue and yellow spotlights. He watches the shifting lights and hears the echo of the amplified narration.

The boys eat and drink what is left at the party. The hostess stands in the kitchen and cries. Above her, the Dolces make love on their bedroom floor, knocking tiles with their knees. Mrs. Dolce's toes are high in the air. Every once in a while she grunts.

The monk reads from the script before him, adjusting the knobs on the light panel to flood the crucifix in greens and pinks. He presses his lips to the microphone.

"The church dates back to the eleventh century," he reads. "It was built by pagans captured as slaves, many of whom died for its grandeur."

Mr. and Mrs. Dolce stand up and smooth their clothing. Mrs. Dolce says they have had a postcard from their son. He will come for Easter, she says, not before. Mr. Dolce shakes his head and walks into his study. He lights his pipe and looks at the books around him. Outside, light fades to dusk and stars appear from nothing.

Romeo's stick catches in the mud. He pulls, but slips. The water feels cool. He lies in the Arno like a dog to drink, his tongue turning blue then rose red then gold.

The Iranian market seller takes Rebecca to his apartment, where leather jackets divided by sheaths of plastic are piled high in a corner, below a poster of John Lennon. In the kitchen, a crucifix hangs over the gas range.

"There are no pictures of Mohammed," he tells Rebecca. "Do you know Mohammed?"

He shows her the pictures of a cancer he has removed, watery ovals of blue.

"Look at that," Rebecca says. "I never knew cancer had a color."

Lise rolls another cigarette, wetting the mouth end with her tongue. She watches as Mario the corn seller rubs ointment on the pigeon pecks that line his arms. He leans against the cypress trunk, an evening breeze quickening the silvery green branches. Lise paints a picture of Mario on a cross, pigeons the size of eagles circling his head.

The boys drive away from the place of the party. They roll down the car windows and stick their moon faces out into the dark. The one who drives says the Arno smells like a toilet. He steers toward the Piazza Michelangelo.

Romeo gets up and taps his stick across the Arno; he walks into the sounds of the city.

The boys lean on the stone wall that borders the Piazza Michelangelo, watching the blind boy Romeo tap his way across the water.

"Romeo! Romeo!" they shout.

"Romeo, look!"

When you're a Jet you're a Jet all the way from your first cigarette to your last dying day, sing the tourists.

Romeo's white eyes roll, then stick, focusing on the round dome of the Duomo as if seeing. The light show nears its grand finale: the monk shrieking, the lights flickering, the stones illuminated blue then rose red then gold, stones brightening as if lit from within, as if coals once on fire are now ebbing, now out.

Rebecca watches from the Iranian market seller's window, the night crisscrossed with other people's clothing: underwear, T-shirts, and socks. Behind her, the Iranian market seller peels an orange, his dark fingers guiding the knife beneath the rind, lifting it from the meat.

On the roof, his roommate sits on a cot, smoking the last bit of hash.

Rebecca will join him. She will sit on the roof until morning, composing the postcard she's been carrying for Marion. You must keep me abreast of everything, darling, Marion had said. This is our world tour.

Guiseppe

1988

Sixteen miles southwest of Verona, the train jerks to a stop, and boys on bicycles appear like birds to a carcass, circling the tracks as an old woman stands at her door shading her eyes to see.

Before this, the football team had run through the station, banging the glass doors of the compartments, scaring Rebecca who sat squeezing her naked knees, thinking of the postcard she had not sent and how she might have written how in Verona an orchestra played at dusk for the men and women who sat at the cafes in the great square drinking. Listen to this, a Pole in Levis had said, and he had played his guitar and for a while she had stood with some others to hear and then she had walked on the Via Menzoni and stopped to listen to two American girls at Juliet's balcony.

Romeo o Romeo, one said. *Wherethefuckartthou, Romeo?*

▾

The old woman who shades her eyes wears rolled stockings and a housecoat and sits in the afternoons to wait for the train from Verona, the passengers looking out to her with the long sad faces and the long sad mouths and the long sad looks of people passing through.

Along the tracks, umbrella pines grow in high thin rows. And on the far side, on the sea rocks where Sirens once sang, sit terns and other seabirds who have come to smell the land. Not so long ago, Sirens rested and wrung their hair in their hands, squeezing water onto the rock to write their names. Now their heads are shorn and they keep to the bottom, watching through the day as the big ferries carry tourists east to Rinzini.

The train, halted, ticks like crickets; the passengers sit still. The boys on their bicycles begin to shout.

In Verona, Rebecca watched the priest walk the cloisters, his claw hands curled on a book, his long black robe trailing the dust on the stones that marked the path of other priests who had walked before. From where she sat, she could hear the orchestra in the square play a Viennese waltz and she could watch as a boy who left school sketched two Italians kissing under one of the stone arches. Not lichen but some green stain framed them: stone mica.

Then the boy out of school shut his sketch pad and stood. He walked down the long stone steps toward the square where the orchestra played, passing the cloisters. There a couple from Kentucky pooled their change to see the unicorn. It reared in the center of the tapestry, like some kind of ghost unicorn, its horn longer than they had seen in books, its white hooves pawing air.

The story went up and down the narrow train corridor, rushing, like some great cyclone of wind, to fill each compartment: the mother had driven her Fiat as close as she could to the stop-gate and sat there within the shadows of the umbrella pines, her baby in the back in its special seat, strapped in, sleeping. After some time, the mother had stepped from the Fiat and slammed the door.

The doctor arrives; he can do nothing but walk the long tracks looking under the train.

Why? Look at that. What're they saying? Thirty-six. Twenty-eight. Younger than that. Very young. A little girl. Look. Sick from love. Sick from no love.

Look.

The Sirens swim up from their depth to see, their bald heads tattooed with seaweed, their strong arms raised to pull themselves onto the flat sea rocks shared by terns and other birds who rise flapping and move on. The Sirens inch their dead legs out and then their feet, grown flat and wide and gray between the toes.

The old woman carries peaches in a basket to the windows of the train, where the tourists try to see and ask who can see and the boys on the bicycles offer what they cannot know. Hiding the peach bruises in her palm, the old woman raises her hand, flattens her hand, as if to feed horses. Rebecca takes a peach, eating it quickly as she leans out the window of the train, her face cooled by the wind that blows through, bending the row of umbrella pines, sweeping them down with a now fierce, from-nowhere force.

The Sirens blow, their teeth cracked and skin burning hot from unfamiliar sun and eyes pale as jellyfish and flat feet itching. Barnacles cling to their elbows and the backs of their knees. A chorus of them sit here on the sea rocks slippery with tern shit, blowing. They make the wind that spreads the word. Beyond them, above them, the clouds. Around them, their sea rocks, the water spreads in fainter circles to a shore coated with petroleum. In the evenings, there will be rainbows and bubbles.

On the train, the ones from Senegal, Egypt, Pakistan, France, Ohio, Switzerland, Russia, Turkey, Colombia, Argentina, California, Indiana,

Guiseppe 1988

Mexico, China, Hong Kong, Greenland, Greece, New York, stand near Rebecca, no room for sitting, feeling the wind that shakes the doors and sweeps the engineer's words up to them, out again, the engineer saying they should stay in their seats and the train will move on shortly.

Rebecca spits her pit out, the old woman watching and nodding and smiling, her black dress blown around the knees. Down the tracks, the boys on bicycles whistle; they have found another piece of her.

The Sirens blow. They are out of practice, their lungs lined with salt. They have difficulty swallowing, and their noses are clogged with the sludge that leaks from the ferries that take the tourists east to Rinzini. They have never been. They have lived near the sea rocks and waited, watching from below the terns and other seabirds land, flight shadows cast down to them like a fleet of black boats, empty hulls they swim into, accustomed, as they have become, to darkness. Their song can lure no faithful now, and so they rarely try.

Rebecca thinks she might begin with this. Tell Marion how the train just stopped and how the sound when the train stopped was like crickets and then silent and the boys on their bicycles kept shouting and an old woman stared and these teenagers whom she met in Verona couldn't really believe that Romeo and Juliet were true and asked her did she believe that whereforartthou bullshit?

The mother had sat on the tracks, her back to the sound of the train's whistle. From her window, the old woman had watched, and, after the train had come through and stopped, she gathered the peaches from the bowl in her kitchen and walked out. The boys on their bicycles had swooped down and soon circled like flies, waiting for the doctor and the inspector and the commissioner and the engineer and the mortician so they could tell them all that they had not seen.

The boy who left school returns to sit in the gardens of the cloisters to sketch the old priest who sits there too, his curled hand useless in his lap, his old eyes closed with leathery lids, his black robe stained from lunches of red peppers in oil. Inside, in the chapel, the couple from Kentucky feed the light box quarters to see again how the unicorn glows. The white of it they can't describe. Milk? Chalk? Bone?

Around them, other tourists read from books, look fast, then walk away, over the stones that cover the bones of monks and heretics. The couple from Kentucky must get ready to leave—tickets to Carmen at eight—but before they go they pour the last of their change into the light box, liking the idea of the unicorn lit in darkness, in the silence of the empty church, alone for no one to see.

The Sirens free her. She rises like a cloud of color, sixteen miles southwest of Verona, and they blow, harder, to send her off. She looks not unhappy; she looks like an ordinary woman dead.

▼

Guiseppe 1988

The priest locks the gate to the cloisters, not seeing how the boy who left school still sits in the gardens, lost in the dark below the rosette that in this setting sun blooms red and gold, Christ and His disciples splintered into pieces of the pie.

The old woman waves as the train begins to move, then she returns home and pulls her wooden shutters closed, lights her lamp. She has a heavy pocket of change, and she will lay out the coins on the oilcloth and count them many times before sleeping.

When the boy who left school awakens, he finds himself alone in the gardens, though in the presence of what? A ghost? The unicorn trembles, not white, really, more ashen, on its four legs. It stands in the place where monks' and heretics' bones have sunk and crumbled to the core, unsteady, its wide eyes purplish, its long snout pale. It stands as it did in the tapestry: surrounded by its own white light and—but for its ink black hooves—brilliant.

Rebecca heads for Rome. She leans against the train windows watching, squeezed into the narrow corridor, thinking of the young mother who did or did not die for love, of her own hands and the grease stains on the windows and the football players running through.

O Romeo, Romeo, wherethefuckartthou, Romeo? She returns to the compartment where she started and settles in across from the man from Amsterdam, the activist who had earlier asked her to sign a petition. You would agree, he told her, if you could understand.

She had signed.

She sees now the list in his lap, his hands crossed over it. He sleeps, his head back against the bank of the compartment seat. Above him are three photographs of Italy framed by a metal band. She leans near the man from Amsterdam to have a better look. The photographs were taken years ago, it is clear. They have faded, but she can see in them what was once there: a church spire in an ordinary square, old men on bicycles pedaling in circles, a woman, her arms around a thatched basket, in a fruit market.

The train lurches a bit, doesn't stop. Rebecca steadies herself. Outside is dark. They go through a mountain, or a hill too high to climb. It is black in the tunnel, the wet walls are close; she can smell more than see them, the musty insides of earth. Then out, again, into the weak light. Umbrella pines cast geometric shadows on the land, truly sienna, ocher. Just as they say. Elsewhere, beyond this arching hill, or closer, there—where the stones define a cluster of houses, a goat shed—may be haystacks and long tables set beneath rambling oaks, flowers in glass jars anchoring white tablecloths that with this new wind whip and flap. Large families gathered for supper.

But they pass through. They speed. The train rocking as it goes. The mother's blood long burned from its wheels, disappeared.

Behind her, down the narrow corridor, tourists sit on backpacks, haunches, speaking languages, exchanging slips of paper, envelope flaps, napkins, notepads with their names, numbers, addresses.

Guiseppe 1988

The man from Amsterdam rolls a bit to his side, lets the petition slip off his lap. Rebecca picks it up. Her name there with the others.

Are you Giuseppe?, she whispers. Wake up, darling, she says, to test the word. Please.

The man from Amsterdam curls his legs up, settles into the hard cold space of the corner.

Rebecca puts aside the list. Finds the postcard, a pen.

Dear Marion, she writes. *Having a wonderful time. And finally, a minute. My Giuseppe is sleeping. Have I told you he is handsome? Have I told you how I met him when he asked me to sign a petition? He is very smart, Giuseppe, and we're on our way. Verona! It was grand. This unicorn* (and here she turns the card around to be sure, then finds her place) *I saw in person. The monks stitched him into the center of a tapestry a thousand years ago. The thread was silk and gold. You should have seen the way he reflected light. Like Mr. Fontaine's head in church.*

There was no more room on the postcard; she had already turned the corner and written upside down.

Your darling, she signs. Rebecca.

She places the postcard in the book in her knapsack. Neruda. Then she leans against the leather bank of the compartment seat and closes her eyes, smelling the damp smell of another tunnel, then the fresher air of the fields they race through. The sun, already, has set, and now the blue hour begins.

L'heure bleue.

She might eat crackers and cheese; she might sit on the back patio and smoke. She pictures Marion, the time she caught her there, turned around awkwardly, as if suddenly struck by the familiar view, a cigarette crushed beneath one white espadrille. This after

Marion had been to the hypnotist, had claimed she'd licked the habit.

"Mother," Rebecca had said. "You were smoking."

Marion turned around.

"Was not," she said.

"I thought I smelled it."

"Wrong," Marion said.

Marion remained briefly defiant, then sat hard in one of the wrought-iron chairs. "I'll tell you what, young lady," she said. "Hypnotists are for the birds. I want a cigarette today as much as yesterday. I can't remember a thing he said."

Marion waved her hand and crossed her legs. She pulled a pack of Virginia Slims from her jacket pocket and lit one, drawing in the smoke and eyeing Rebecca.

"Go ahead," she said, letting the smoke out. "Say it all at once, quick as you please. I'm up to here. Between you and your father I'll have a heart attack before I'll drop dead of cancer. Life is life, after all." She took another drag. "Isn't it?"

Excuse me, Rebecca hears.

The man from Amsterdam, the activist.

"Could I have that?" He points to his list. "I need that," he says. "We have to do something."

"We do," Rebecca says, returning the list.

"Did you sign it?" he asks.

"I did," she says.

They sit across from one another. He doesn't look the way she pictures Giuseppe. He is too dirty; his hair needs a wash, and she would like to shave the blond stubble from his chin. He wears a vest, colorful, and around his wrist is a piece of string.

"Did you forget something?" she says, pointing to it.

"Yes," he says, serious.

They sit moving with such speed, through tunnels, past towns on distant hills.

"How long have you been traveling?" she asks, polite.

"Today?"

"No."

"Oh, that." He shifts in the seat. He is the type of man with whom she will always feel too organized, too clean. She has packed light, but neat: T-shirts of various colors, walking shorts.

"Going on, I don't know, twenty-three months?" he says, rubbing his eyes, as if he had to see the number.

"Wow," she says, stupid.

"You?" he says.

"Seven weeks. Well, here. Seven weeks. I only like it here."

"Italy?"

"Yes."

"It's good, true. Have you been to Cologne?"

"Germany? No, God. I couldn't."

"There's a cathedral."

"Yes?"

"You didn't bomb it."

"Right," she says, thinking, wrongly, of Dresden.

She bites a nail.

"So you're alone?" he asks.

"Yes, today. Well today I am. Before I wasn't. I mean, I traveled with my friend. Giuseppe. He had to return. I mean, I'm meeting him." She smiled. "You?"

"I'm Wilhelm," he says. "Are you meeting him in Rome?"

"Excuse me?"

"Your boyfriend. Are you meeting him in Rome? Is that where you're going?"

"Yes, I mean. Yes."

"You'll like it," he says. He unwraps a sandwich, looking at her. He offers her half, but she has had a peach. He turns to the window and eats. She would like to read, or perhaps to write another postcard, but she looks out the window too, as if he needs company. Then down at her hands. She feels bored in the way that she often feels bored alone. She is a single woman, older than most single women she has met on her trip, nearly thirty, not a backpacker, no longer a student, a woman who worked for a while, who lives on her own in New York City. This is the way she explains herself. She needs to explain, at first. They all do: where they are from, what they do, who they are or are not meeting. They huddle together on cots in a hostel. In Portofino, five women. She can't remember their names.

"I saved for this trip," Rebecca told them. "Whenever I got lonely or something, I would think about this trip. I mean, I saw myself here so clearly. I saw myself in all these places I had read about. And somehow, in other places, I looked different. I felt different. I had a different life. I don't know. You know?"

They nodded. They were all friends, fast friends, in the way women become fast friends quickly. They have talked all afternoon. They are coincidences, five women who share the same room in a cheap hostel that rents cots, that requires you sweep in the morning, that offers only cold showers. They don't mind. They will spend the night. One or two may stay longer. Rebecca will not. She will talk with them until morning, and then she will leave, again, alone. This is in Portofino or Genoa, in Milano, in Orvieto.

Guiseppe 1988

"Anyway, I worked at this newspaper. There were all these men who worked there—the writers, mostly men—and they would just hang out, around me, and talk to me. They all had wives but always seemed, I mean. Interested? I live in this studio alone; sometimes a guy will move in. This is the way it was while I saved money. I typed. I mean, that's what I did at this newspaper. Typed, and edited sometimes. Input. What I like to do is take pictures, but this was good money and it wasn't bad, particularly. These guys would hang around, just hang around my cubicle when they weren't playing rotisserie baseball. And then this woman came to work there and she was a knockout. Really. And the guys kinda shuffled over to her cubicle. All of them. And I found myself suddenly sort of looking up and seeing air. And these few things I had tacked up to the walls, the partitions of my cubicle. You know, things that somehow meant me. A fortune cookie or a napkin from some restaurant. One of those colored paper parasols. And I thought, this is my life? So I just blew it. I quit the job and took the money I had saved and here I am."

The women nodded. They were inside a large masonry building, one that had once held prisoners. Tiny windows let in light from the streetlamps, but mostly it was dark.

"Same with me," one of them said.

"What?" Rebecca said.

"That's exactly what happened to me."

"You know," says Wilhelm, turning back to her. "You remind me of some American actress."

"I do?"

"The one with the teeth, the big teeth."

"Mary Tyler Moore? People always say Mary Tyler Moore."

"No, no. With the teeth, the big teeth."

The boy who left school feeds the unicorn bread from his knapsack, his palm flat out as he has learned from feeding horses. Beyond the locked gates, far from here, the Pole in Levis plays for the heroin addicts who have gathered in the square where the orchestra earlier played, and elsewhere flutists in their starched white shirts have joined violinists for veal—they spear lemon, careful not to squirt the priest who sits beside them eating. And on the other side, in the place we must wait to get to, Sirens scratch their feet and wiggle their toes. Soon they will slip down again and wait for the terns to return and the early morning ferry to rock them asleep in its wake.

But first the moon must rise. In its light, Rebecca watches at the window, Wilhelm gone. The train gains speed. The mother who sat on the tracks has been forgotten by the passengers, who sleep and dream of other things, who smoke in the corridor or in the bars of the cities they have stepped into.

In moonlight, Rebecca sleeps and wakes, sleeps and wakes, travel weary, her forehead pressed against the glass. At times, she believes she might see more than landscape—what Giuseppe would have shown her, if he were here, if he hadn't gotten off in Bologna, if he didn't wait in Rome. A wisp of something. What?

▼

Dear Giuseppe:

At work, before, the boys would lean against my partition, into my cubicle; they would feel entitled to that. It was enough to send me home. Vertigo or PMS, I would say, and split. To my studio. I'd walk as fast as I could. I could do that. Walk home. And I had this leather bag, black, that hooked onto my shoulder, and black shoes and my stockings I would roll down and off as I went. I didn't care. I looked like all the girls who didn't care.

Outside my studio, cats fought, and at lunchtime the stock guys from Wall Street, the traders, would shoot heroin in the alleyway between my building and the one next door. I could look out and see them, their ties on but tossed over their shoulders like architects do when they're drafting, or fathers when they bend to tie their children's shoes. Their hunched white starched backs.

Sometimes, I'd jimmy open my window and yell "Hey boys," as if I were one of those breasty singers from a USO tour and these were my boys, my troops. Then, I can't remember what else.

Sometimes, one would look up and wave, as if I'd caught him peeing, but most times no one bothered. It might have been the cat fights—they might not have heard me at all.

The cats sat near the boys, beneath the window of the floor below mine, the illegal Chinese restaurant's kitchen, where the illegal Chinese sliced fish meat off bones. The cats would wait beneath that window, one behind the next. There were a dozen of them at least. Cats and Chinese. At night both would sleep on the floor of the kitchen, sometimes spilling onto the stair landing so that if I came home late I'd have to take a big step over them, holding onto the banister, my good shoes in my hands. I always took my shoes off when I came into the building, so I wouldn't make much noise. I had this idea that any night a policeman would step out from the shadows and snap handcuffs onto my wrists. It was illegal, all of it. I don't know what was supposed to go on there, but what did was not. The Chinese. Me. The guy on the floor above me who sculpted metal.

There were things I liked to do. For instance, I liked to take photographs of altars, or the things people built to remember something. I called them altars. Most of the people I found building these things were homeless; they would spend their day collecting what they could find, then put it together on an abandoned lot somewhere in my neighborhood. There were a lot of abandoned lots around, most of them covered in half-bricks and broken glass and automobile parts. These were not the altars. The altars were what you would find in the corners, or in a circle in the center. From a distance, they would look like junk, but if you watched these places you would see the person returning to add to what they were making. Sometimes the altar would just be in the arrangement of a few pairs of shoes. But once, in an empty lot between two buildings, mostly hidden from the street and choked with trees, I found about a hundred teddy bears, all different sizes. Natalie, the woman who made it, wouldn't speak to me, but her friend told me she had been in the camps.

After a time, I decided I needed my own altar, so I set up a table inside next to the window and let the dust collect there. I let it collect for months. I never cleaned that table.

Across from my studio was a park, and sometimes I would sit there, on one of the iron benches, and watch the squirrels tunnel in the paper bags. I would think maybe all of this was an altar of some sort, that we were in some kind of arrangement we couldn't get far enough away to see. I hoped for that: an order, a system.

I talked to one of the boys at work about it. He was a married man named Hugh who wore suspenders and liked to smoke. He would ask me to join him on the roof, where the company had set out folding chairs and an ashcan. Hugh and I were there one afternoon—the place was some sort of wind tunnel, and to talk involved shouting— and I asked him about this, about order, about system. Hugh had the reputation of being very smart. Some past relation had designed the Chrysler building, and his father had been involved in restructuring Mexico's debt. Often, when he would lean against my partition, he talked of drawing rooms and important visitors. Of trips. He seemed to know things. And so I asked him.

"What do you think, Hugh. Do you think there's a system to us, any pattern here?"

"The matter?" he said, squinting into his cigarette smoke. "Nothing, really, just feeling a bit blue."

Around us were the top halves of all the famous buildings, but they had outlined the edge of the roof with boxwoods, as if we weren't sitting in the middle of New York City twenty-seven stories in the air, but actually on Marion's back patio, our feet firmly on the ground.

"Well, I'll spill it," Hugh continued. "It's Patricia."

And so on.

Patricia was Hugh's wife, but she wanted out. Then something about his sons and how his father had never been present at any of his birthdays. It didn't matter. On the roof or sitting in my cubicle, the boys *leaned*, spilling secrets. I was required to sit up straight.

I read Neruda. I read Neruda out loud and paced around the studio, sometimes yelling the one about the iron, the one about the lamp.

Such order in things. At times, one of the Chinese boys would be there too, sitting propped up on my bed, his hands open at either side. When I reached the end, he would nod and pat the empty place next to him.

I went to synagogue; I liked the shape and the patterned tiles. But there was no singing and I needed singing. I went to church, 10th and Fifth, next to the offices of Forbes magazine. I had been in there once, to see the collection of Fabergé eggs. I had passed through the foyer, where the portrait is: Mr. Forbes senior in oils, ten feet high, his motorcycle behind him, his helmet under his arm.

I told the boys about it at work. Of the Fabergé eggs I remembered nothing, but that painting I could describe in detail: the black leather jacket he wears, his big important glasses, the gleam of the sun off the helmet, red. The boys had seen it, of course, knew exactly what I was saying and more. They interrupted, as boys do.

In church, I sang. I took communion. I did not hold the wafer under my tongue, but crunched it as I do cough drops. Afterward, I felt calm. I walked to Washington Square Park and squatted beneath the arch. NYU types were filming something; people walked dogs. It was a sunny day, and the fountain bubbled. Then someone tapped me on the shoulder, a small woman, a dwarf. She had legs that bowed out, like a Fabergé egg, and short blonde hair in a Dutch boy cut. She was half my height when I stood.

"Come on," she said. So I followed. She walked me around the side of the arch, to a tiny door that you wouldn't notice unless you were looking. She had the key to the door and opened it. I followed her inside the arch and we climbed three flights of stairs up to the top landing. Another door led out to a small balcony at the top of the arch. There we were, above everything.

"Lift me up," the woman said. So I bent down and made a cradle with my hands, as you do to help someone onto a horse.

"Thank you," she said. Below us, a parade was passing by, a children's parade. Some of them seemed to be dressed as Mexican bandits; others wore long skirts and carried flowers. Mothers, or women who could have been mothers, walked on either side of the line of children, which snaked around the park where the joggers usually jog. Someone held a sign I couldn't read, and a motorcycle led the way—a bullhorn propped on its handlebars blaring a tinny song, vaguely Latin.

The parade seemed to lasso all the other people in the park, and they came together, from our view, as if a constricting pupil in one eye, giant, black. They stayed near the fountain, watching the children.

My arms ached, I felt hot. I wanted to lower the woman, but thought that would be rude. Her gnat-yellow hair smelled of dandelions, weeds she might have rolled through on her way here, a hill she might have tumbled down, using her dwarfness, the thickness of her legs, her head, to her best, as a centipede will if touched. I pictured her rolling, rolling, somewhere near the Hudson. Rolling all the way to Washington Square Park, unrolling just beneath the arch to be taken up—who knows?—by someone bigger.

It was like the time I made Thanksgiving for the Chinese boys. They brought litchi nuts and I basted a roaster. The cats howled and I threw them the gizzards. I had tablecloths from Marion, things she had packed and sent, along with boxes of Cup-A-Soup and a few odds and ends from her utensil drawer, a note that said *Wish you were with us* inside a smiley face. She had also included a ceramic frog I remembered from one of her continuing education classes: green with long purple spots.

I decorated my studio with white Christmas lights. The place was all windows, and late at night, when the illegal Chinese were lounging on the floor, stuffed with stuffing and speaking their language, and I, apron intact, lay on the bed, thinking in mine of Thanksgivings past when Robert, standing at the head of the table, would say a prayer around the table, a storm came up and shook the windows and blew out the electricity, so that all at once, instantly, the white lights went out.

What could it mean? I had no answers.

I suppose I was looking for a husband. This I told Hugh, who got a kick out of these things. Later he would say, Found any fish? when he leaned into my partition. I took up his smoking habit, so he would always invite me to the roof. I would follow his wide back and the tweedy flaps of his jacket riding high on his rear as he climbed the stairs and opened the heavy fire escape door. In the summer, the boxwoods were at their greenest, and somebody had planted geraniums in clay pots and lined them up in an even row.

Hugh and I had spent one lunch hour going to Woolworths to buy proper, better chairs. The folded ones we folded and put away. Our beach chairs we left in a circle, pink-striped and welcoming. "Hello little chairs," Hugh always said.

"Hello," I would say back in a chair-voice.

Hugh lit a cigarette for me and then one for himself. We sat facing south, toward the World Financial Center, our legs out on the gravelly surface. If we looked straight, we would see only boxwoods, but looking up we could see the towers.

"There," Hugh said more than once, pointing at them, "is the new center of the world's finances."

"Exactly," I said.

"A lot of fish at the center of the financial world," Hugh said. He tapped ash into his palm. "Whole schools of them."

"Groupers," I said. "Bottom feeders."

"My wife," Hugh began. "Came from a flashy school of fish. Tropical. The kind you see in those stores. Her family were none too pleased to have an ordinary trout in their midst."

"No such thing as an ordinary trout."

"All right. Then catfish or something. I don't know."

"Catfish is good. I once went catfish fishing in north Florida. It looked just like a mud hole, and this old guy I was with made his own poles out of bamboo and used green peas as bait. We pulled them up by the dozen."

Hugh wasn't interested. "They near ran me out," he said. "I had to come begging. From that moment, Patricia had the upper hand."

A siren went by below, loud as if we were on the street. I stubbed out my cigarette in the ashcan.

"Back to the grind?" I said.

Hugh looked at me; he had those eyes men sometimes have.

"But we haven't talked about you. The fish," he said.

"Fish smish. It's dull, all of it. Tomorrow, I promise."

And so it went. Until Hugh stopped smoking and I quit my job, tired of the boys leaning, of the memos in and memos out, ready to see the world. On my last day, the boys surprised me with a party, a flat cake and wine on the roof. They had tied streamers to the box-woods, pink and white and blue, as if this were a baby shower, and the day, windy, picked up the paper and spun it around and around so that the streamers looked like big tentacles waving in the air.

"Look at that," I said to Hugh. "I caught an octopus."

Before I left New York, I took a new friend out to lunch. He was a survivor of Buchenwald and he knew Natalie, the woman with the teddy bears. He had been hanging around when I photographed her altar—a wiry, old guy with bad breath and a few stands of hair combed over his head. His name, Joseph, seemed wrong for him, but he insisted on no Joe.

I took him to a quiet place, not so many customers. I wanted to hear what he had to say, about the camp, about the Nazis, about what they did to him. I wanted him to put me into the middle of a drama, of a story with a beginning, middle, and end, with good guys and bad guys and Mozart thrown in. I wanted him to tell me what I should know before leaving, before setting out. Survivor's guide to surviving, and so forth. But he didn't want to talk about it.

"Come on, Joseph," I said.

"Nah," he said, pointing at the pickle on my plate. "No good. I have nothing to say. Are you going to eat that?"

After I paid for lunch, Joseph nodded and stuck a toothpick between two of his teeth. "Obliged," he said. He pushed back from his chair and shuffled out in front of me. Then he stood on the street corner and wrote something in his little notepad. He was in the habit of jotting things down. Comments on service, he had told me. In Germany, he said, before, he had been a hotel manager, and that was his business. He wrote in his little notepad with a golf pencil, then he pushed the pad back into his breast pocket. When he looked up, he seemed surprised to see I still stood in front of him.

I had a sister once, or a sister was once born. I have heard little of her—something went wrong with her heart and she lived for only a few days—but in our family she survives, constant in her absence, as if she took with her certain letters from our family alphabet. There are words we can no longer pronounce, gaps within them, whistles, holes that leave us breathless, beached.

Around the time she was born, I learned of the roundness of the world. I would lie on the shorn grass of our front lawn and squeeze my eyes shut, believing I could feel it turning, revolving on its axis. The feeling began in one foot and worked its way up my leg, the leg that felt heavier, that initiated the turning. The turning! As if I were in a sideways Ferris wheel or some kind of grinding machine. Hands weighted on either side of me to the wet grass, I pretended that if I opened my eyes I would wake up on the other side, in another country, one of the countries where girls were engaged in serious conversations wearing wide-brimmed hats with yellow ribbons, or one of the countries where girls sat holding the hands of sick children in long white hospital wards, or one of the countries where girls sailed on ships beneath harvest moons, the kind of moons, Marion had told me, that meant it would never rain.

This was where I was when my father came home to tell me she had died: on the front lawn, my arms out on either side of me, my eyes squeezed shut. My sister had been born several days before, and

I knew that my mother would not bring her home until she grew hair. This is how my father explained it: once a baby girl grows hair, she's allowed to go home, he told me. Not before.

And so I'd been waiting for her, for Marion, for a dinner at home instead of with the neighbor. My father usually returned after visiting hours, after I'd been put to bed in our house. He would come to the door and wait to see if I were sleeping. I would say good night, to let him know I was not, and he would come in, sit next to me in bed, hold my hand for a minute, then kiss me and leave. This night had felt different, though, and long after I had been put to bed, long after I saw him stand against the light from the hallway, then heard him move down the hall to their bedroom, I stayed awake. So when the telephone rang, I heard it. And I heard him leave, again, not bothering to close the door quietly.

I went down the stairs, one hand on the banister, the other holding up the long trail of my nightgown, a yellow one I had found earlier in a paper bag on the kitchen counter, one that belonged to my mother, I assumed, though I had never seen her wear it. I opened the front door slowly, stepping out to my place on the lawn. It was an hour I had never before witnessed. There had been rain—the forsythia were still heavy with it—but the ground was already dry. Mist rose. I lay down and shut my eyes, waiting to feel the turning of the world, the pleasant motion.

But something had changed. I knew it somehow, felt it immediately from the ground up: a terrifying sensation. Falling. I fell. I reeled and spun. As if, between the time I had last tried my trick and now, the world—wound too tightly—had been released. Now the motion pinned me, knocked my breath out. I couldn't breathe, the air rushing through the rip my sister's death had made in us, in our landscape, in Marion, in Robert. I knew it then before I was told, felt it somehow and wanted to flee, to cheat it, to lift above this house, our house, and our neighbors, above the garage and the dining room Marion had painted green, above my bedroom upstairs with the horse-covered quilt, above the streets and trees, and higher still, until I got to the whispery height of the clouds, the moon, my nightgown my camouflage, yellow, another star. I wanted to be gone before they returned. The house empty as it would become for me. "Hello," they would call. "Hello?"

"Goodbye," I would yell from my great height. "Goodbye."

But the turning held me, and though the speed of the world subsided somewhat in the days and weeks that followed, the absence did not. Letters dropped out. Words were stippled, useless.

Robert disappeared to the basement, where the dollhouse begun for me before the baby was born remained in pieces on his worktable. Marion came home for a while and lay in bed; then she left, again, to spend weeks at a camp by a lake for men and women who needed peace and quiet. This is how Robert explained it. "She needs patching," he said.

When we picked her up, I understood. Though she looked whole enough, she was hollow as an imposter: someone had scooped out her insides and given us back a Marion balloon.

The day I left my studio in New York, I stopped at the door to the Chinese kitchen to say goodbye to my friends. "Hello?" I said, and some of them appeared through the steam. They began to clap, so more appeared, all of them clapping and speaking at once, their words like the first great clattering of blackbirds in spring, hopeful.

Your friend,

Rebecca

The train pulls into the Rome station. Rebecca folds her letter to Giuseppe into an envelope, licking the flap and pressing it down hard. *Giuseppe,* she writes where the address should go. Then adds, *Mr.*

She is tired in the station, has had no sleep. She steps out and looks around her: a square, pigeons, and a postcard stand just as in Florence, Verona. For a moment Rebecca wonders if she hasn't traveled south at all, but in fact has looped around to where she started.

She heads out, walking toward the first tobacco sign she spots, down a narrow street where the smell of automobiles is strong and men stand at bars drinking espresso. They've parked their motor scooters on the sidewalks, and she must maneuver around them. Sometimes they call out to her. "Good morning, Miss America," they say.

She stops at the tobacco shop and buys a bus ticket. Then she continues until she finds a bus, empty, idling, the driver reading a newspaper.

"The Vatican City?" she asks.

He nods and she steps in, stamping her bus ticket and sitting in the back on one of the seats that stretches the entire length of the bus. In time, other people get on, and eventually the bus driver lowers his newspaper and restarts the engine, driving the bus slowly, turning down narrow streets until they get to one of the wider avenues. There are fountains, spraying, twisted marble men, and angels holding up green palms, arrows piercing white breasts. Rome. Everywhere, light on stone.

The bus swerves and climbs, and then Rebecca can see the walls of the Vatican City, the dome of Saint Peter. Somewhere walks the Pope, his robes black, his white hands doughy. In St. Peter's Square, she steps off the bus and shoos away the gypsies, who bump up against her, pat her, looking for bills. It is all in her shoes and there is not much of it. She will leave, she knows, in a few days, find her way back to New York. Begin again.

But first, the steps. The final place: the basilica, the Pietà, Michelangelo.

She ascends. Around her the tourists have sunk to their knees. Jesus behind Plexiglas, draped the whole length of Mary, slipping off her lap. Rebecca gets as close as she can, curls her hands on the aluminum rails that set him apart, boxed, plastic-sheathed. God, he is, or a close relation. She thinks of the Chinese, the way they sometimes looked as she watched them sleeping, their small hands flattened beneath their heads for pillows.

"I've got to find a mailbox," Rebecca says to an old man who stands next to her. She sees now that he is selling something, plastic figurines of Jesus on Mary's lap, slipping.

"This is a separate country," the man says.

"I've got to find a mailbox," she says.

"You need the right stamp," he says.

She nods. "I have it."

"Good," he says. "This has a separate code; it's a separate country, all of it. It's not Rome, it's not what you'd think. It's a triangle. You could walk, I could show you, in less than an hour."

"No," she says.

"It's somewhere else. You can't explain it," he says. "Would you like a guide?" he says.

"Yes," she says. "No, I mean. I want a mailbox," she says, "please."

He points the way, not so far, and she goes, climbing the travertine stairway to the gift shop. Inside, stacked in rows and rows, are the plastic figurines of the Pietà, and clear globes of the Vatican City that snow when you shake them, and the Pope on porcelain ashtrays. She looks at the rack of postcards of the Pietà and finds several choices: Mary's face, nose intact, chiseled, marbled, her round eyes shut, or lowered, so they look like two round white stones, the kind you might find at the bottom of a clear stream and think beautiful until, having pulled them out and dried them in the sun, you see that they are not at all extraordinary; or Jesus, his eyes open, looking up at Mary. She picks Jesus and takes Him to the counter to pay. The woman gives her change and tells her the mail slot is around the corner.

She leaves the gift shop and finds one of the benches that line the hallway that leads, the sign says, to the Sistine Chapel—temporarily closed, with thanks to the Nippon Corporation. She sits and pulls Giuseppe's letter from her knapsack, finds a pen. On the back of Jesus she writes Marion's address, then Dear Marion. She reaches down and fingers Giuseppe.

I ditched Giuseppe, she writes. *We're on our own.*

She stares at the words she's written, trying to picture Marion's reaction, what the day will be like when she receives it. Warm, surely. It is always warm in Baltimore. Blue sky. Fields of daisies. Marion will walk down the driveway, as is her custom, her feet crunching the gravel. When she reaches the end of it, she will open the mailbox, one she decoupaged years ago, when she had run out of other things to work on. Now a turtle sits squarely on the rear of the box, its eyes wide open.

Rebecca balances the postcard against her Neruda book, steadies her hand. *Love,* she adds, *Rebecca.*

She holds it out in front of her, as if needing to read it from a distance. Then she brings it close, kisses it, and shoves both letters into the mail slot.

New York

1988

R ebecca is pretty. She has the kind of face made beautiful with makeup—round black eyes. She lives again in the city, now east, in a rented studio in a neighborhood of artists and crack dealers where women her age paint their lips red, cherry red, like Audrey Hepburn in *Breakfast at Tiffany's*. Everyone is trying to be Holly Golightly.

Rebecca wants to care for something passionately, or give the impression that she does. She reads a bilingual edition of Neruda and checks the Spanish words against their English translations. She listens to Irish ballads sung by trios of long-faced women and hums the tunes behind the tweed partition that separates her desk from other desks at the place where she works.

She has taken a new job editing children's primers. "All day long," she'll tell a person she just met. "I limit my vocabulary."

This is a clever thing to say and people laugh, but it is also the truth.

▼

When she can, Rebecca jogs around and around a balcony track, listening to the thud of the basketball bouncing below. There's a buzz of fluorescence shivering over the world, and all of the players who have passed through its glow are reeling and whirling in the light. Or so Rebecca imagines.

She looks down on the court, watches as the men leap and shout, smacking hands, rear ends. When it's over, she knows, they will total points and determine the winners.

After running, Rebecca walks through her neighborhood thinking pleasant thoughts. This Marion taught her to do for nightmares. Think pleasant thoughts, Marion would say, meaning Rebecca should picture a field of daisies, or sunflowers.

Once home, Rebecca watches television in her studio. On it now is a special about the blue whale. The blue whale, the narrator explains, mates for life. Rebecca had known about loons and certain types of ducks, but never about the blue whale. She watches the screen as a male and female blue make their way to California for the winter, crossing miles and miles of distance speaking a secret underwater language.

When the blues are almost to Marin, her friend Victoria calls.

"I've got somebody who wants to meet you," she tells Rebecca. "I told him you were tragic."

Rebecca watches as the blues rise and spout.

"What does he look like?" she asks.

"Cute," Victoria says. "Smart. His name is Kevin. He majored in English."

"Does he play sports?" Rebecca asks.

"I don't know, probably," Victoria says.

"Basketball?"

"Maybe. Is that a problem?"

Rebecca combs her hair in the mirror of the Ladies Locker Room. Here, she feels young, uncomplicated. It's a good feeling, a summer camp feeling.

Empty Kleenex boxes and plastic bottles and hairbrushes and hair dryers crowd the counter. Warm air blows out of a dirty grate. Near where she stands, someone has hung a poster of a naked man, his muscles shining as if oiled, his hair wet. TRUST, the poster reads.

From around the corner, a stream of old ladies appears, their breasts flat to their rib cages, their gray hair wet. Rebecca has seen these old ladies taking a class in the swimming pool in the basement. She has watched as the ladies reached their arms over their heads, carefully mimicking their young leader, keeping their chins above water as they grasped the poolside with free hands. Rebecca had pictured them under, their gray hair waving with the tides, their mended skin a blue-gray white.

Think pleasant thoughts, Rebecca thinks.

Perhaps Kevin will call soon.

Rebecca is pretty. People tell her so. She has small breasts and small hips and a stomach smooth and flat. Sometimes at night, alone in her studio, she presses her palm against certain places of her and pre-tends that her palm is the palm of a lover, his finger.

When she does, she listens for her lover's breathing, but what she hears is the sounds of the men who live in the park across the street, their voices—guttural, indistinct. The men burn fires in the trash cans to keep warm, the glow from the fires reaching Rebecca. At times, when the wind shifts the steady flames, the glow from the fires seems a glow from a moon.

Kevin calls. His voice isn't bad, deep with a tremor of humor. He may be smiling. Rebecca tries to picture him as she's talking, but what she pictures is the guy who works at the deli on First Avenue, the guy who never looks up as he counts out her change. She has talked to this guy a few times, but still. Each morning when she goes in to buy her cup of coffee, he looks past her as someone would look past a stranger.

Kevin sits across from Rebecca in a restaurant of his choosing. Behind him, a black net webs brick—a conch shell, a star fish, a plastic shark. Kevin has spread his napkin over his lap before ordering; he has sipped the wine and approved.

Now he looks at Rebecca.

"I am an athlete," he tells her. "Victoria said I should mention it."

"Oh," Rebecca says, smiling.

"The trouble is the city," he continues. "I mean, sometimes I feel like a panther in a cage, rrrrrr, get me *out*, you know? I could end up like one of those crazies shouting fuck in the Laundromat—"

Rebecca listens to Kevin for a while, then finds herself wondering if anyone could still hear the ocean in that conch shell.

"Excuse me," she says.

She goes down the stairs to the basement, where the waitress has pointed out the ladies room. On the door someone has written Ladies and/or Gentlemen.

A draft rises from the bathroom floor. Beneath the sink, what looks like a carton of dead lettuce has been stashed.

Rebecca splashes her face with cold water.

Marion told her once that men think in lines—from point A to point B to point C—and that women think in circles, from the point at which they started, back to that point again. Rebecca tries to remember the point at which she started, but all she can think of is something from Neruda, *Let us build an expendable day.*

Then something about oranges.

Rebecca splashes her face again, wipes it with one of the rough paper towels from the dispenser. She gives her lips another coat of red.

I am trying, she thinks.

The players breathe quickly, breathing in the glory of the afternoon. From the far windows, the sun bears down in holy beams. The players have wrapped their ankles, hardened their muscles with weights.

Underneath the court, in the cafeteria next to the swimming pool, the old ladies work the cash registers and serve up mashed potatoes.

Later they will clear the tables for bingo, admiring the paper plate drawings from the class for retarded adults on the cement walls.

Rebecca runs.

That morning, Kevin kissed her back, told her she had an incredible body.

She pictured two half-court games of five-on-five; twenty men jumping.

"Thanks," she said.

Morning rain has turned the city gray. Rotting garbage blows like tumbleweeds through Rebecca's neighborhood—the wind sour. Someone has vandalized the front wall of her tenement building, writing words, or rather, white letters put together as if words, across the brick. The whole thing illegible. Nonsense.

Rebecca pictures the vandal a woman her age, a woman writing a secret language—a language understood only by one other. Somewhere. This is what Marion has promised. You're, what? Twenty-nine? Thirty? You've seen the world. Been everywhere, darling. It's a different generation. Whoopie! she said, rubbing her toes. They sat on the flagstone patio drinking wine.

"It's not so easy," Rebecca said.

"Fiddlesticks," Marion said. "There's plenty of fish, etcetera. Not like in my day. In my day the first one that ogled you got the prize. Your father might have been an ax murderer for all I knew." Marion sipped her wine and let the garden catalog she had been reading slip off her lap. "I believe you will make your mother proud. So sue me, etcetera," she said, stretching out her legs and yawning. "Yours will be perfection."

Rebecca tries to read the graffiti, but the sentences the woman writes are complicated poetry, indecipherable. Obfuscated for the point of obfuscation. Hermetic. Shut. She edits nothing out of them— they go around and around and around, like eternity, Rebecca thinks, picturing this vandal as herself.

Rebecca kicks Kevin out. It has lasted several months.

She kicks him out as he exercises on a floor mat in the middle of her studio, his shoes next to him, men's sneakers sized fourteen, their tongues curled over their laces.

"We are like two people standing back to back, glad the other is there only for the balance," she says.

"What?" he says, sitting up.

"You have no idea what I think, no understanding at all," she says. "Do you know that the blue whale hears through its skin?" she says. "Do you know that it knows? I mean it hears. Leagues away even. In separate oceans."

Kevin looks past her. "Not like plankton," she continues. "Plankton are drifters. That's us. You, me, Marion, Robert. That's the point, really. Isn't it? We are plankton. We," Rebecca repeats, "are plankton."

Rebecca jogs around and around the indoor running track, counting the times that she passes the solid yellow line. Each day, she pushes herself to do ten more laps. She feels that if she can reach the next increment of ten she will somehow be rewarded.

161

Below, the players shout out their garbled sounds. They push and shove. Beneath them, in the basement, the old ladies grip the poolside, their white legs floating, weightless.

Victoria calls.

"Kevin is heartbroken," she says. "He thought you were perfect. He loved your studio."

"It didn't work," Rebecca says.

"Well," says Victoria. "That happens. Anyway," she begins. "I was thinking. I met somebody last Saturday, and I thought you might be interested. He lives in California, but he's here now for a while."

"Oh?" says Rebecca.

"Tell me if it's too soon, but I was thinking," says Victoria. "He was an art major. Berkeley. Now he sculpts. Stone, I think. Anyway, I told him you were in something you were about to get out of. I told him where you live. He loved it," Victoria says. "He loved the whole thing."

A better day today. The sun shines on the men in the park, the ones who light fires in the trash cans at night and in the morning stand at the corner, eyeing the girls. The girls walk to work, prettiest now—their hair washed and combed, their stockings pulled up to their waists, their leather jackets zipped. They have dressed themselves as carefully as their mothers once dressed them, their lips painted red, cherry red, like Holly Golightly in *Breakfast at Tiffany's*. They are on their way.

Rebecca joins their general direction. She walks quickly, determined, picturing, as she goes, the new one coming for dinner, picturing him leaning close, holding his hand against her back, carefully, listening, understanding her secret language.

Tomorrow morning they will wake up early. He will sigh to have to leave her.

And after he has gone, she will wash the wine stains from the well of their wineglasses, rinse the dinner plates, dress. Then she will set off again, only this time the sun will rattle the tenement windows, the wind will be fresh, and the deli guy will smile as he counts out her change, pressing the silver coins to her palm, like communion wafers to believers.

Istanbul

1990

In Istanbul, a spotted cur slinks through the room where the faithful go, circling Mohammed's hair—a curling simple thing no bigger than an eyelash, a wish in glass—licking hands. Down the hall, the slippered Sultan steps, his silver toe points clicking the tile, click click, click click, click click.

The Harem hear him. Dunking to the bottom of their swimming pool, they hold their breath for sixteen counts, their bound hair curling loose from tightly twisted braids unraveling out to green-blue water where, above, the minarets rise to guard the last stop on the Bosporus.

"Never so afraid, Richard the Lionhearted turns back," reads Rebecca. Tom has wandered off. Husband, she thinks. My husband has wandered off. They are on their honeymoon. It startles her to think the word.

In Cambridge, New York, the nuns of New Skeet make cheesecake. Their Brothers down the muddy road train shepherds, German, purebreds pacing smelly cages, pink tongues rolled in fangy mouths, the saliva beaded on their black gums dripping to their matted manes of burr and cum and thorn.

Tourists walk the muddy road and peer into the darkened window of the Brothers New Skeet Dog and Gift Shoppe.

In Clay, Missouri, the Sisters of the Forgotten Order station themselves for prayer, revolving around the bony unfleshed feet of old Saint WhatsHerName. The story goes that they brought her here from catacombs in Rome. A wagon pulled by horses carried her. Taken from the belly of a ship—whose sailors, seeing banana trees, canaries, pastures good for grazing, stepped into the black Atlantic— the Saint was saved by pirates, then bartered to a cowboy name of Nonesuch; he was looking for a change in luck.

Nonesuch took her as far as Missouri. That he dumped a Saint in Clay plagued him as far as California.

In Rome, the curs dig deeper, grunt; their wet-pink muzzles rooting out the smells of truffles, rotting flesh, skunk cabbage, crust crumbs, chocolate in the pockets of the monks who wander through the darkened catacombs. The Brothers forget poor Michelangelo, who labors on the Sistine ceiling almost blind. Pope WhatsHisName has sealed him in to find the face of God but oh, poor Michelangelo, his beard curling around and around like Neptune out of water, come to judge the quick. The dead-tired Michelangelo, flat on his back, his eyes glued nearly shut from lack of sleep, his brush between his broken teeth, his thumb up, seeking out relief—too close, he is. But this is not about proportion. The Sibyls grew ten times their size. His enemies took wings. Moses looks like his lover's father.

Thinks Michelangelo, all I can do is try my hardest.

In Istanbul, Constantinople, the Harem stays under, their fanning eunuchs fanning faster, stirring the green-blue water up, their black and peering faces broken by the stir of it into a thousand.
The Harem holds for eighteen counts.

And still, around Mohammed's hair the faithful circle. The spotted cur licks. Some tourists are particularly pungent: Tom, whose fingers smell of breakfast rolls; Rebecca, bleeding.

She shoos the thing off. "Get," she says.

"Blue Mosque?" Tom says.

"Get," she says, pushing at the wet-pink snout.

"Blue Mosque?" Tom repeats.

"All right," she says, and turns, her heels clicking the tile, click click, click click, the cur's nails clicking close behind.

"This dog," she says once in the heat. "I'm up to here."

Tom cleaves a band of dark-faced children, barefoot, offering up their shoes, their bracelets, beads, postcards, figs. "Miss America. Miss America," they call to Rebecca, but she pushes past the gates into the square.

In Cambridge, New York, the nuns of New Skeet go to and fro, talking of Amaretto, Chocolate Chip, classic Strawberry. Prayers are first, and then the baking. Ovens are stoked, as strong hands keep kneading. The dough must rise before the Sisters pound it down again.

In Clay, Missouri, the Ladies of the Forgotten Order have come undone. The heat's been off for days. The Sisters' lips are turning blue.

Who will hear their prayers?

They fax the Vatican. A busy signal.

We have to save ourselves, they say. Who's got any good suggestion?

Raise money, somehow. Bring tourists in. They'll drive to see the caves in Carthage, the roller coaster in Jerusalem, the car show in Bolivar.

How can we compete?

They pray. Please God, they say. We need a vision in this land-scape. Something to make a wonder out of wheat.

My real sister, who lives in New Haven, one says, says Jesus is there, outside of Frabbrizio's Funeral Home. He's in the sycamore, a thing to see, his feet that thin, just like in all the pictures. She says you can't even find a parking space.

Please God, they say. We need something a little similar close to home. In our spruce, maybe. Or possibly the ash.

In Cambridge, New York, the shepherds pace their cages while the Sisters slice some smaller pieces for the Brothers who could stand to lose a little weight.

▼

Istanbul 1990

In Istanbul, Constantinople, Rebecca, bleeding, steps into the darkened Blue Mosque, a Kleenex on her head. In time, she sees the prayer mats, edge to edge.

Think of all this emptiness as sculpture, Tom tells her.

She squints, but cannot see a thing. The light is all, a blue light coming through the tiny windows, a crown of thorns around the mosque's bald head. *L'heure bleue.* What had Marion said?

"I'm leaving," Rebecca whispers into emptiness. "It smells like feet."

Outside, she sits on a bench with other tourists, listening. In Istanbul, she has heard voices, loud ones, rising in what might be her epiphany, borne, she believes, from these new words: wife, honeymoon. Nonsense, Tom says. You think everything should be a religious experience.

Around her the barefoot boys cluster, begging for a hairbrush. She hasn't one, she tells them. Please, they say. Cigarettes?

Niente, she says.

They turn to a couple with matching shorts and hats who sit down on the bench adjacent to Rebecca. She has seen them before, every morning as she and Tom sit for breakfast, sliced tomatoes and yogurt, some sort of fig jam, in the hotel garden. The couple, they have noticed, look almost exactly alike—their hair cut the same length, their shoes of the same durable leather, their socks pulled to their knees.

Must be Brits, Tom had said the first time they saw them. Brits always end up looking like each other.

Now Rebecca smiles, but the couple does not see her; they are lost in the cluster of barefoot boys, who have persuaded them to empty their pockets.

▼

In Rome, the Cardinal knocks upon the Sistine Chapel door and yells that he has brought the genius Michelangelo his supper.

"Feed it to the dogs! The dogs!" the genius Michelangelo is shouting.

In Cambridge, New York, the tourists knock on the darkened window of the Brothers New Skeet Dog and Gift Shoppe. In time, they ring the bell. Inside, a brother flicks the light switch and opens the door.

"Yes?" he says.

"Can we look around your gift shop? Do you have the pumpkin flavor?" the tourists ask.

Puppies scramble at the brother's feet, jumping to catch the crumbs that sift down from his fingers.

"Of course," he says. "Come in, come in."

In Rome, the faithful gaze straight up to see the colors cleaned of all that smoke. The chemicals they used! Financed by the Japanese!

No pictures please.

Click click. Click click. Click click.

Many of them lift their faces there to God, or is that Adam?

For four quarters, others listen to the voices speaking English/Italian/Russian/Japanese: *What you are seeing is the greatest work of art in the history of mankind, completed by the genius Michelangelo in record time, without food, in an uncomfortable position, which eventually resulted in a goiter.*

Tourists wearing earphones crane their heads and listen, cameras hung around their necks like crucifixes.

▼

"Is he for sale? Can you train him?" the tourist asks, pointing at the one with black around its eyes, a villain's mask.

The brother nods, his rosary slung beneath the hugeness of his belly.

In Rome, Michelangelo is nearly finished—His ears, His eyes, His whiskers. The final touches. Beneath him, in the farthest corner, the spotted cur laps up his dinners—forty days and forty nights worth, rooting out the meat, the bone, his fangy mouth now thick with potato, corn, speckled color on his fur, pigment dropped from higher places—greens and reds and blues and pinks—his mane a masterpiece.

In Istanbul, around the curling hair the faithful circle, guessing about Him from this: Blond or red? A lisper? Handsome? Hunchbacked? They will talk until morning of it. On the shining Bosporus, the ferry heads for port. Russia a stone's throw, Tom reads.

"Imagine that," Rebecca says, not looking.

From here, ahead, the minarets are swords, a circle plunged into a sky that, in the ferry's turning back, has darkened quickly to gray, rain clouds weighing on the city, on the palace locking fast its door. The spotted cur will sleep alone; the guards have cleared the faithful out.

And on the deck, above the seagulls beating backwards for a fish gut, Rebecca hears silver toe points clicking as they pass the empty palace grounds.

Tom steps out of the Blue Mosque, smiling. He holds up the camera and gestures for Rebecca to stand. The light is good behind you, he says. She turns to see. The setting sun has made the city wall pink. The smell is of gasoline, car fumes. She coughs, turns back to Tom. Gorgeous girl, he says, and clicks.

She smiles too late.

A man selling kabobs from a cart pushes it over the cobblestones and onto the better road toward downtown; a bear in chains disappears in the back of a pickup; an old woman winds through the central market, seven straightback wooden chairs tied together with twine and hoisted on her back.

Tom sits beside Rebecca.

"How would you feel if we got divorced," she says to him.

"What?"

"We could get divorced, or annulled or whatever it is, then just keep living together. We wouldn't tell anybody."

"Why?"

"Because they would think we were nuts."

"No, why would we do it in the first place?"

Tom has big hands and a face that reminds Rebecca of a child's face. She has loved him since the first minute she saw him, ascending a staircase, his big hand on the banister.

"To not be married," Rebecca says, sitting up.

"You should have thought of that last week," Tom says. He holds the camera in his big hands on his lap.

"I did," Rebecca says.

"Well, now what?" Tom says.

Rebecca shrugs. She takes the camera from his hands and holds it out in front of them, turned toward them, her finger poised. "Cheese?" she says.

▼

Tom is too far away to hear Rebecca's apology. She tosses it up as she would a bread crust to the gulls, says it against the wind. "I'm sorry," she says. She would like to apologize to all of them: Marion and Robert, Tom. She has done something terribly wrong, she knows. Something she should repent. But she isn't sure where to go, whom to pray to, what to say. She hears voices rising in no epiphany, only confusion, repeating Marion's wishes.

Think pleasant thoughts, Rebecca thinks. Keep your mind trained. Look out to where the crowd is looking. There is so much you might miss. Richard the Lionhearted was never so afraid, but you will not turn back, no. Just look. Look! These empty palace grounds, still maintained as they were at the height of this once great civilization.

Ithaca

1992

The hat, Rebecca recognizes: Marion's hat. Ordinary brown felt, nothing particularly grand or *stylish,* a hat to be worn on a train: brim bent from frequent transfers, years spent wrapped in tissue paper, usefulness in question. It is among her own things as she unpacks, unrolling glasses chocked with last week's news. Arranging. Rearranging. Tom calls this new apartment their rooty one. *Finito,* he says. Next time they're carrying me out.

Marion eventually stopped wearing hats. Too poodlish, she said, a word she got from Rebecca. Still, Rebecca tries the brown one on, light from the window spilling over the mirror onto the freshly painted wall—a frenzy, as if the wall is water. Rebecca stares into the lake. Narcissus. What was the story? The man who turned into a flower; the flower that turned into a man.

Outside, clouds come down, leaden, one-dimensional. Snow is predicted in New York, a blizzard of stupendous proportions. Everyone waits, holding their breath.

Rebecca releases hers slowly. I can still get out, she thinks. I should be going, really. It's still too soon to try. A burden or blessing this biology. I'm, what? Thirty-three? Thirty-four? I have time, really. I should be on my way. Take the train, twelve dollars in my pocket, velvet dress, gloves, Marion's felt hat.

"I'll just split," Marion would say. "Mexico, or maybe back to Indiana. I could finish my degree." This after white wine and melba toast on the back patio. Marion began her pledge of leaving, as far as Rebecca could remember, soon after their move to Rochester; she kept it up all the way to Baltimore.

"I've been thinking of going, really," she said. "No more talking— just packing my bags, writing your father a note, taking a plane." Rebecca sliced the sharp cheddar. "Would you loathe me?"

"I'd get over it," Rebecca said.

Marion wore buff sandals, her nails painted with Coppery Peach. She had that day invited Rebecca to join her in her cocktail hour. White wine, solely. Sharp cheddar on melba. Seventeen years old is old enough for wine, beer, and cigarettes, if you must, she said. But don't let me catch you with the hard stuff for at least a year. Rebecca already felt slightly drunk. She was home from boarding school, where she got drunk quite often, but here she felt a different, sadder drunk. A grown-up drunk. She looked hard at her mother, who had let her gray hair grow down to her shoulders and wore it back in a headband, a cardigan sweater draped around her shoulders, cocktail rings clicking glass as she fingered a smudge.

"It's so nice to have company," she said, pouring more for both of them. "I miss you in your faraway place. Are you having a wonderful time?"

"Wonderful," Rebecca said, lifting her glass, spilling a bit of wine on her jeans.

"Me, I'm stuck," Marion said. "Mexico, I don't know. Indiana, for God's sake. Promise me something, darling. After you graduate, you'll send me postcards? You'll have a wonderful time?"

"Rebecca?" Tom says. "Hello?" She looks, again. He stands behind her, his big hands at his sides, his little glasses dusted with sawdust. Around his waist hangs a toolbelt: hammer, screwdrivers of varying sizes, tape measure. He looks rugged, a cowboy with pistols. Normally he works with water, water slicing stone. A sculptor, Tom, a monument builder.

"Where were you?" he says.

Rebecca takes off Marion's hat.

"Here?" she says.

"Why don't you sit," Tom says.

"On what?" Rebecca says. Cardboard boxes form a kind of pyramid in the center of their living room, news on the newly sanded floor. A nest, this. Rats, mice. A den. They have been here for one week and still, every time Rebecca unlocks the door and steps in, she wants out. Tom doesn't seem to notice. He builds a new room, a talisman to optimism, he says. Something for a baby. He nails pale birch plywood into a cube he plans to stain a deep red. A hat box for a *petit chapeau.*

"On me," Tom says, sinking to one knee in a gesture Rebecca last saw the afternoon he proposed. Then she had looked at him with difficulty, as if staring directly into the sun. "Maybe," she had said.

▼

She finds other Marion things among her own, wrapped in the same tissue, packed by the college boys she hired to pack Perry Street: postcards, letters in a box marked This and That, a kelly green coat on a padded hanger, the Japanese wooden bowl with stamped flowers, a first-place trophy from a mother-daughter Ping-Pong championship—Underwood Elementary School Champions, Rebecca and Marion Clark, May 16, 1967, ceramic animals, hollow—some containing rusty paper clips, pennies, sixteen-cent stamps, a cloisonné ashtray, hand towels embroidered MCP, a yellow nightgown, an ebony cigarette holder, dirty white poker chips, a half-finished needlepoint sampler reading *Of All The Things I've Loved and Lost I Miss My Mind the Most.*

At first when the packages arrived, addressed in Marion's hand, Rebecca had protested. What did she need with the detritus of that life? What shore was she?

Tom sleeps. Sawdust in his ears, his eyebrows, on the soles of his feet. Rebecca does not. She looks through *This and That*—Niagara Falls. Tokyo. Virginia Beach, Virginia—a mother atlas. She fingers Florence, why shouldn't she? David, his perfect legs, perfect shoulders. She might have lived in the place where the farmer stuck his hands down the pig's throat, blood to his elbows, and the just-graduated boy danced with the farmer's wife, the candle dripping, sealing their seduction trail in wax. Late afternoons, the long Uffizi windows reflected pigeons startled from their roosts on Neptune's neck; boys on motorbikes raced into the Piazza Signora, stuck their hot feet in the fountain, and raced on. She watched from her place at the Caffè

Boboli table, farthest to the edge, the others empty. Italian women passed, their high heels clipping the stone square. They wore sunglasses and lipstick, skirts tight to the knee. Rebecca drank a lemonade and smoked.

Dear Marion,
Having a wonderful time. Wish you were here and so
forth. It's just what you would imagine. Even the boys on
motorbikes. I have met some interesting ones. A guy from
Naples named Giuseppe. Handsome, smart. He is madly
in love. Tomorrow we're off to Venice.
> *Love,*
> *Rebecca*

Rebecca had admired her signature, the look of the words, the sound. Gay and free; her mother's daughter. Then she had licked the stamp and signaled to the waiter for the check. The waiter, a young man with a white cloth over his arm, walked slowly over and stood as Rebecca counted lira.

She looked up and smiled. "Is your name Giuseppe?" she said.

"Sure," he said.

Dear Marion,
Having a wonderful time. Athens is not at all how you
would picture it. Did you know the Parthenon was never
supposed to be white? The book said pink, which made
me laugh, wouldn't you?
> *Love,*
> *Rebecca*

Outside, the blizzard begins, snow falling sideways, flakes minuscule. The city slows to a halt, traffic lights staggering green, yellow, red. It is too late to be walking, but a young woman, newly arrived from Haiti, crosses Hudson going west toward Washington. Because she is newly arrived and because Hudson is practically deserted and because the few taxis idling in wait have lighted off-duty signs, she stops. In the middle of the street, the young woman leans back, opens her mouth, catches snowflakes on the tip of her tongue, wishing she could hold them there, save them for her mother who, ill with gout, bitterness, wished for snow, the taste of it in her own dry mouth, parched, this same night, from wanting.

Dear Marion,
Having a wonderful time. Thought you might like to see
where I'm staying. It's there (see arrow on front), in the
back. I have a view of a place where a miracle occurred.
No one seems to be able to tell me what miracle, though I
believe it had something to do with a unicorn. C'est la vie!
Love,
Rebecca

Rebecca feels Tom's arms, his big hands, around her.

"Where are you now?" he whispers, his breath warm against her.

"Thinking," Rebecca says. She stands at the window, watching the snow. "Snow always reminds me of Mrs. Aberly, the one who was having the affair with Mr. Curran. This was in Pennsylvania, I think, though it might have been Delaware. Anyway, everyone knew about it. In church they sat next to each other in one of the back pews, holding hands beneath their coats. Only in winter. God knows what they did the rest of the seasons."

Tom massages Rebecca's shoulders. He would like to interrupt her, to stop her ceaseless worry, but he knows not to.

"I caught them once," Rebecca is saying. "Kissing. Outside, behind the church. I don't remember all the details. We were playing hide-and-seek and I ran into this forsythia and there they were. She had these gloves on and that's what I saw; he had on a winter coat, and her gloves were up, around the back of his head."

Tom's hands touch Rebecca's face. "Come to bed," he says, turning her into him, squeezing them into an awkward match.

Tom sleeps, his light snoring lifting Rebecca up, setting her down again. She has tried all of Marion's tricks: thinking pleasant thoughts, picturing a field of daisies. But no.

Useless, thinks Rebecca, her cold feet slapping the newly sanded floor.

Dear Marion,

Having a wonderful time, etc. Thought I should use up this paper. So here I am. Sans Giuseppe. Where? Not sure, exactly. In foreign waters. Somewhere between Palermo and the one-horse town I just left, on a boat, on a body of water which I couldn't name. The sky looks like something I might have seen in the Uffizi, a fresco of a sky in need of MAJOR CAPITAL IMPROVEMENTS. Cleaning, for one. Think of all that cigarette and cigar,

*factory, campfire, battlefield smoke of the centuries. And
simple hot air. But I don't imagine anyone could
construct a scaffold that high that would hold.*

How did I get on to this?

*I met someone my age who quotes the Bible. We were
staying in a former convent so it seemed oddly
appropriate. She had a tiny copy of the book that she
kept up her sleeve. She was full of fortune-cookie wisdom,
one-liners that seemed prophetic, that you wanted to
believe.*

"What are you doing here?" she asked me.

*It seemed a question I should have a reasonable
answer to.*

"I don't know," I said. "Looking?"

*"For what?" she said, her eyebrows tight, her hand up
to loop her hair behind her ears.*

"Salvation?" I said.

*She asked me what did I mean. What did I mean by
salvation? But I hadn't meant my own. She said children
are birds let loose in the darkness, errors renewed.*

*This is what I mean by quoting from the Bible, but she
said no; she said it was from a novel she couldn't
remember the name of.*

It has been years since such a blizzard. On the television, weather
maps show a white swirl foreign as cancer. It sweeps across the north,
descending on Minneapolis, Pittsburgh, Rochester, New York City,

waving its serendipitous tail. Hello? Goodbye? People attempt to keep warm, strive for cheerfulness, exultation. Still, cars careen into snowbanks. Cattle disappear in frozen lakes. Electric lines go down, sheathed in ice; entire families are separated by circumstance: children in school basements, mothers in attics, fathers between the office and the airport.

Yet somewhere, boys and girls skate on a frozen blue lake, arms out, heads back, cracking the whip, the older ones going two-by-two, their thrusts synchronized, their newly sharpened blades slicing the white ice as thinly as paper slices skin. Others hold the bigger hands of siblings, stretch their legs toboggan-length, flexing toes in furry crusted boots.

Tom wakes to find Rebecca breathing over him.

"It's still snowing," she says.

"Is it?" he says, sitting up. "I'm asleep," he remembers.

"Let's do something," she says.

Tom rubs his eyes and reaches for his small glasses on the bedtable.

"Rebecca," he says, hooking the wire stems behind his ears.

"Please," she says. "Surprise me."

It is close to four A.M. when Rebecca and Tom reach the base of the Williamsburg Bridge. They have skied across Broome, down Crosby, through the empty streets of Chinatown, the city still as stone.

Travertine. Tom unearthed the skis he had secretly purchased for such an occasion, for a surprise—skis waxed to a gleam, tips curved like Indian slippers.

"Voilà!" he said, revealing them.

Rebecca was wearing Marion's hat, Marion's kelly green coat.

"Are you serious?" she said.

"Why not?"

"It's two in the morning."

Tom looked at her.

"Carpe diem," he said.

"I don't have my winter things," she said.

"Look fine to me," he said.

"This?"

"Nobody's out there; no cars, no anything. It's beautiful, Rebecca. Look."

Can you picture her? She's taken off Marion's hat, tossed it on a snowbank. She is warm enough, even hot. She pauses at the bridge rail to catch her breath; looking out toward the river, Manhattan. She has never seen a landscape so diminished, so absolutely trapped in black and white. She stands and watches, wishing Marion alive, wishing she could write to her of it: *You should have seen us,* she would write. *We were having a wonderful time.*

The snow tapers to larger flakes, melting on Rebecca's eyelids, her lips; she tastes them, fingers pink with cold.

Ithaca 1992

Dear Marion,

Only one more. Letters do me in. Having a wonderful time and so on. Belgium a bit cold, overall. Gray. Too many recent battles. This is the place where both sides saw the rider on the white horse. You remember that story, don't you? The Germans and the French, or maybe the Germans and the English. Anyway, the rider simply walked his horse down the middle of the battlefield and everyone stopped shooting.

This city is full of little girls in hats. Everywhere I see them, playing hide-and-seek, gathered for games, sitting on benches with their nannies, waiting for the bus. The hats are straw or felt or ribboned, the girls uniformly beautiful. Yesterday, walking along the canals—that's all there are here, bridges linking bridges linking bridges to other bridges, a metaphor for something—I thought of that hat party you made for my eleventh birthday. Do you remember?

We were in Charlottesville. My first all-girl party. You said you would make me a dress from any pattern I chose, so we went to a fabric store downtown. The salesman wanted to know the occasion, and you said, her birthday. Eleven, you said, and pulled me closer into you, though I was too old for that. You held up ten fingers. She's off my hands, you said. How will I survive it?

The salesman looked up from his cutting as if wondering whether you wanted him to seriously consider

the question, as if you might believe that after the guests
went home you would just sulk into the woods and quit
breathing.

   Then he shrugged. You will, he said.

   They kept the patterns in the back in what looked like
card catalogs, worn wood files, dull brass handles. We
looked through the junior teen book, each dress sketched
over a stick figure of a girl, lean and tall, blonde or
brunette, and chose something, you scanning the rows
for the right drawer, your rings clicking against the
wood.

   At home, I unwrapped the skin-colored tissue paper,
unfolding arms, waist, connecting all those pieces as if it
weren't my dress I was constructing but me. Once
arranged, it took some time for you to pin them together,
but then you held the tissue dress up to me, its sleeves
fluttery, its skirt billowing. You will be beautiful, you said,
as if you had just seen an apparition.

   I accepted the prediction without question.

   The hat was mine to decorate. I glued buttons and
yarn, things I had picked out in the notions department.
A mesh silver net hung over the brim in the way I had
seen in magazines, a ribbon, thick and green, glued to the
stiff straw. A garden creation.

   But the hat came later, after much fuss over the dress.
Still without its zipper, its hem, you now slipped it over
my head. We were alone, the new house charged with its
usual unfamiliarity: shadow corners, noises in the rain
cellar, scratching beneath the piano. Trees I'd never climb

*cracked in winds we had no idea the direction of. Here
we are again, but where? East, south? Do we speak with
an accent? Should we curtsey hello? That might be the
smell of salt on the air, are we near an ocean?*

*We would unpack our boxes, place our books in our
bookshelves, our things—the wooden bowl from Japan,
the cloisonné ashtray with its hairline crack, the cherry
table you bought for a lark—throughout the house,
against walls hung with prints, photographs from other
places. Here we are, then. Here we are, you'd say.*

*I stood in your room as instructed, listening to the
dishwasher rinsing. It was past my bedtime, but you
made a special allowance; the next day I would turn
eleven and I could sleep as late as I wanted. Of course I
would wake before light, open my eyes to find the dress
pressed and ready on a hanger, my polished Capezios
beneath it, tights draped like a shawl around its
shoulders.*

*But for now it's still in pieces, loosely stitched and
pinned into a vague teen form. I'm not worried. You will
stay up through the night to get it exactly right, to finish
in time for the arrival of my guests the next day. Now you
need to see if you have cut it correctly, if the shoulder
seam is flush with mine, if the sleeves hang too far past
the wrist. I stand in your bedroom next to the card table
set up with your old Singer, my arms at my sides, my hat
temporarily perched on your pincushion. For a moment I
am in the dark and then I'm not, the dress slipped over
my nightgown. You reach for my hat and place it back on*

my head, then you step out of the way so I can look in
your mirror.

 Can you picture me? I am almost off your hands.

Tom's big hands cover Rebecca's eyes. "Surprise," he whispers. "Don't look." She does not, turning into him, awkward. Behind them their tracks are filled in with fresh snow, no trace. Rebecca feels Tom's hands pull away, then opens her eyes. He has dropped to the snow and scissors his arms and legs. His eyelashes are white with snowflakes, curls dipped.

He stands, again, smiling: the angel momentarily clear, its wings raised as if waving. Hello? Goodbye? Rebecca pulls Marion's coat tighter around her shoulders. It is too much, this happiness.

"I'm thinking of leaving," she says.

Tom stands in front of her, listening. "Where?" he says.

Rebecca shrugs. She has no idea, really. "Ithaca?" she says.

There will be moments when your life becomes clear to you, Marion said. Times when the damn book falls open, and you read, I don't know, a sentence, a word.

She waved her hand in the air, brushing something away.

Gnats, mosquitoes. A heavy rain. Trees dripped water onto dead leaves. September. This in Baltimore, or Durham. In Houston, Philadelphia, Charlottesville. Rebecca, next to her, will soon return to school, or another city, the new one she has moved to, or will leave from. Rebecca on her way, the train departing, the whistle blown.

Tom is looking at Rebecca in the way that he will, as if she is granite and he cannot find the form. It strikes her suddenly what he might see: Marion, both women in perpetual eclipse.

She shivers, smells the sharp scent of mother against the cold: tobacco smoke, perfume, powders of unnamed variety, mints, dirty nickels, dry toast, Chablis.

"Rebecca?" Tom says.

She looks at him.

"I wish you'd stay," he says. His glasses are fogged, his breath white; she pulls him toward her and kisses him, her hands on either side of his head, the warmth there, his David curls. Is it as simple as this?

Too soon to say. She's, what? Thirty-four?

She releases him, moving on. Poles, glides, poles, glides, ascending the bridge.

By midmorning the East Side is jammed with cars, standstill. Messengers with cardboard squares on their backs weave in the traffic, everyone dismissed due to weather complications. Students in loose jackets, ears plugged with headphones, loll in doorways, subway entrances, at countertops, watching. A bus jammed with people, most weakly sitting, lumbers up Sixth. Rebecca rides in back, next to a mother whose boy repeatedly lifts and lowers himself by the bus strap. The mother holds the stem of a lamp, its shade wrapped in brown paper. Rebecca watches her, the boy, the tediousness of his repetition.

The mother sees Rebecca looking. "He has this thing about flying," she says, by way of apology.

At the Port Authority, she buys a ticket. Ithaca. The name beautiful. She knows what is there, but it sounds Greek, promises Greek. White. Pink: the blue grottos, just beyond Ithaca, someone told her, and a lake turquoise-colored. Caribbean. Having to do with limestone. Sediment. Glacial patterns. She gets in line with the soon-to-be boarders, waiting.

There will always be bus stations, train stations. Airports with bright lights buzzing, hot tarmac. Travelers. There will always be fluorescent bulbs, fly strips. Suitcases. Wrapped sandwiches. Dogs beneath wheels. Dirty windshields. Sticky countertops. Fingerprints. Naugahyde. Folded umbrellas. Appetites. A dog barking. Pickups. Yellow lines. A road block. Chickens. Brick and mortar. Pickaxes. Weather.

Rebecca takes a seat, the bus surprisingly full. Her neighbor breaks her sandwich, eats.

Rebecca turns in the other direction, composing a postcard to Tom. The bus starts, swirls down the circular, shell-like gangway. A journey. All of them must feel the surge of it, the promise. Isn't it all they ever wanted: to move on, to pull out, to fly?

Ithaca 1992

Dear Tom,

This shouldn't surprise you. This doesn't surprise you,
does it?

Love,

Rebecca

She might write a longer letter, but she doesn't want to confuse
him. An interruption, this is. A change. Change from crisis.
Khrassilys. Greek.

Excuse me, her neighbor, interrupting. I'm not going to eat this.

I'm sorry?

Pickle?

No. Thank you. No, thank you.

Tom has understood. Tom will understand.

How far? says the neighbor. Rebecca smells the sharp smell of
pickle, trying to remember.

Ithaca?

The neighbor raises her eyebrows, intentionally. In this weather?

Rebecca shrugs. Can't be helped.

No, says the neighbor. I guess it can't.

▼

Rebecca reclines in her seat, the bus driver announcing that the video will begin, momentarily. They tunnel through the weather, watching.

Excuse me, says Rebecca's neighbor. I'm getting off.

Of course, Rebecca says, turning to let her through.

Good luck, she says, dragging her bags.

Thank you, Rebecca says. Rebecca watches her go, passing through the red warming lights into the Sheraton lobby.

The bus cleaves snow as a ship would white water, the current strong, its direction determined by, what? The moon? The sun? Now there are so few. Travelers. Most have gotten off, stepped down, found their places, other places, though still, they continue to dream of snow, of white water, ships. They might make love, drink warmed milk and cognac, snip a tomato from the vine and stop to think, their hands, fluttery at their throats, buttoning their buttons, tying shoelaces, their hearts, quickening:

What became of us?

They arrive in Ithaca in the late afternoon, the bus pulling into the bus station, crunching snow. The bus driver turns off the engine, swings the lever that opens the door. Here we are, he says.

Rebecca gets out with a man. Last stop. The man disappears quickly, someone there for him. A taxi idles near the handicap space, exhaust in plumes.

The bus driver honks, waves; he has turned the bus around and pulls back onto the road, the bus shrinking beneath a flock of geese flying, honking over; the sky a dull gray.

Rebecca opens the taxi door. Blue grottos? she says.

Now? he says.

Why not? she says, getting in.

Children shovel sidewalks, front stoops; the streets are lined with bare trees—sycamore? linden?—snow shadowed, thickened in outline. A few neighborhoods, then a shortcut through town, the driver pointing out certain important landmarks: the movie theater, the department store. Most windows are boarded, plywood planks over doors—as if a hurricane is expected and everyone has buckled down. Soon they're out, again. That's it? Rebecca says. Ithaca?

These days, he says.

Rebecca stares out the window: a billboard for McDonald's on the horizon. She is not sure what she expected: something close to Chartres, perhaps. Tom had been before, sketched buttresses, etc., spent a term learning stone. He told her what to expect. The blue she would remember, and the children: red-cheeked choirboys late for mass, goosestepping through the snow like twelve black crows, their leader— the priest, the storyteller, Zeus—in tow. Thirteen then. Christmas. They had come for mass. To celebrate decisions made, Tom said. To inaugurate the possibility of a *petit chapeau,* Tom said. To ask God for His blessing.

God is here? Rebecca had said.

According to someone, Tom said. They drank coffee at the cafe across from the cathedral. Tom read the guidebook to find according to whom, and Rebecca looked out the picture window: the little boys, the leader. Thirteen blackbirds. Christmas pie. The bells ringing then— or, no, that's Notre Dame. No matter. They went inside, and by the time they had—up the long aisle to find a pew, the miked priest mouthing words they didn't understand—the choirboys and their leader were securely in front, their eyes closed as if to more vividly picture God. But, no. She knew. They pictured their fingertips, numb with fumbling, they pictured their socks soaked through, their shriveled mouse-pink toes.

But arriving! Arriving! Chartres so suddenly on the horizon, off the unbroken line of the highway, reward for distance crossed, pilgrim's prize! Brilliant as angels tumbling from a broken sky. Look, they had said. Here we are!

They have turned off the turnpike and now go through a series of labyrinthine turns, an unplowed road, a forest of sorts, the taxi skidding this way, that. Finally, the driver stops. Rebecca looks. A log cabin. A sign in the window reading, Welcome. Another reading, *Closed.* Everyone already elsewhere.

This is it, the driver says.

The blue grottos? she says. The lake?

He gestures with his thumb. Around that trail. You'll see it. The kids ice-skate there this weather.

Ithaca 1992

Dear Marion,

*Having a wonderful time. Ithaca is not at all how you
would picture it. But did you know the Parthenon was
never supposed to be white? The book said pink, which
made me laugh, wouldn't you?*

Love,

Rebecca

Rebecca walks through a fractured wood: tree limbs broken
letters, words jumbled, rearranged, sentences read in mirrors, backwards, split syntax, splintered; stories revised; her "damn book," as
Marion said, impossible to decipher. Or is this a moment? There are
a thousand ways to read it: How Rebecca Found Her Husband,
Again; What Went on in the House of Rebecca. How Rebecca Took
the Bus to Ithaca. The ending or the beginning. Rebecca listens hard,
language creaking in a new wind; clouds blow in, snow falls again.
The sound overwhelms her, creaking, groaning, opening, closing: a
thousand doors she might walk through; a thousand rooms in a
thousand hotels in a thousand places, lobbies where drunks play
pianos still, where women in pearls sit at small, round tables drinking
crayon-colored aperitifs, hotels at seasides where she might rest on
a wooden bench bleached by sun, seaspray, the sky stormy, the
weather unusually cold. She stays in her hotel room, the French
windows open wide, the misty air coming in with high tide so that
she must take the extra blanket from the top shelf in the closet,
scratchy wool, red and blue striped, and drape it around her
shoulders.

▼

Rebecca sees the blue lake, dusted white, and, nearby, children sitting on logs in front of a small fire. It is near dusk, the sun low. She walks toward them. She has always loved their company. The children look at her. How Rebecca Approached Children. The boys wear red hunting caps, the girls pink mittens clipped at their wrists.

I forgot my skates, Rebecca says, clapping her hands. The girls look around, as if they believe she might have lost them. One girl stares straight at Rebecca. I've got some that might fit you, she says.

She is the kind of little girl you might meet on a movie line, or at the local swimming pool. She wears a beret, dark blue, and though she is mittened there's no doubt her fingers are slender, her nails bitten to the quick, a fleck of pink polish on each from an arrangement she wanted no part of, perhaps an all-girl party, a sleep-over. She has a spray of freckles, easily counted, across a delicate nose in need at the moment of blowing, and dark eyes that immediately remind Rebecca of Tom's eyes. No matter. There will always be little girls.

Rebecca thanks her, sits down on the log and takes off her shoes, understanding, suddenly, that she is terribly tired, that she has come a long way and has no idea of the outcome: What Happened to Rebecca at the Lake of the Blue Grottos. That she has gone means that she must return, will return, the circle eventually finding its beginning, the dragon biting its tail. What had Marion said? Women go in circles, men go in straight lines. But look at this now: the lake, even frozen, pure turquoise, a hard blue diamond, a gem.

Rebecca cinches her laces tight, then stands, unsteady: a woman learning to stand. The children forget her, even the freckled one. They move on to other games, building snow forts, assigning teams. The snow is falling more heavily now, difficult to move through, and still, Rebecca goes. It's been years since she last skated. With Marion, it was, on the pond in the woods behind their house, the last one, near Baltimore. Marion held onto her hand so tightly, wobbling, telling Rebecca to go. They were having a wonderful time.

Rebecca now glides, cutting the ice as neatly as paper cuts skin. Unsteady, then not. She goes faster, surer, weighted as she is. She skates a figure eight forward, then backward. She circles the lake, her ankles strong, her legs stronger. She feels exhilarated, light. She feels entirely elsewhere: How Far Rebecca Went. She might look up to the hills and see sun through blue glass. Chartres. Or the pink of the Parthenon.

The children leave, their toes wet, bones chilled. The freckled one will remember her skates tomorrow and return to find them, laces tied together, a chocolate from Rebecca's bag in each toe, frozen.

Rebecca is alone. She continues, steady, eyes closed, arms out, palms up, fingers open. She pushes on, gliding, circling fast and then faster, the blades cutting ice, through snow heavy at time, at times tapering. Can you picture her? Rebecca disappearing, reappearing out of white.

THE AUTHOR

Claire Holt

KATE WALBERT

was born in New York City and raised in Delaware, Georgia, Texas, Pennsylvania, and Japan. She has degrees from Northwestern University and New York University. Her fiction and articles have appeared in numerous publications, including *The Paris Review, DoubleTake, Fiction, The Antioch Review, Ms.,* and *The New York Times.* Walbert also writes for the theater, and her play, "Year of the Woman," has been produced at the Yale School of Drama and at Villanova University. She is the recipient of a grant from the Connecticut Commission on the Arts as well as fellowships from MacDowell and Yaddo. She currently lives in New York City and Connecticut, where she teaches writing at Yale University.